3/21

HAMILTON-WENHAM
PUBLIC LIBRARY
Hamilton, MA 01982

LENDING THE KEY TO THE LOCKED ROOM

MISSHITSU NO KAGI KASHIMASU

Paul Halter books from Locked Room International:
The Lord of Misrule (2010)
The Fourth Door (2011)
The Seven Wonders of Crime (2011)
The Demon of Dartmoor (2012)
The Seventh Hypothesis (2012)
The Tiger's Head (2013)
The Crimson Fog (2013)
The Night of the Wolf (2013) (collection)
The Invisible Circle (2014)
The Picture from the Past (2014)
The Phantom Passage (2015)
Death Invites You (2016)
The Vampire Tree (2016)
The Madman's Room (2017)
The Man Who Loved Clouds (2018)
The Gold Watch (2019)
The White Lady (2020)

Other impossible crime books from Locked Room International:
The Riddle of Monte Verita (Jean-Paul Torok) 2012
The Killing Needle (Henry Cauvin) 2014
The Derek Smith Omnibus (Derek Smith) 2014
The House That Kills (Noel Vindry) 2015
The Decagon House Murders (Yukito Ayatsuji) 2015
Hard Cheese (Ulf Durling) 2015
The Moai Island Puzzle (Alice Arisugawa) 2016
The Howling Beast (Noel Vindry) 2016
Death in the Dark (Stacey Bishop) 2017
The Ginza Ghost (Keikichi Osaka) 2017
Death in the House of Rain (Szu-Yen Lin) 2017
The Double Alibi (Noel Vindry) 2018
The 8 Manor Murders (Takemaru Abiko) 2018
Locked Room Murders (Robert Adey) 2018 (bibliography)
The Seventh Guest (Gaston Boca) 2018
The Flying Boat Mystery (Franco Vailati) 2019
Locked Room Murders Supplement (ed. Skupin) 2019
Death out of Nowhere (Gensoul & Grenier) 2020
The Red Locked Room (Tetsuya Ayukawa) 2020
The Thirteenth Bullet (Marcel Lanteaume) 2020

Visit our website at www.mylri.com or
www.lockedroominternational.com

LENDING THE KEY TO THE LOCKED ROOM

Tokuya Higashigawa

Translated by Ho-Ling Wong

Lending the Key to the Locked Room

This book is a work of fiction. The characters, incidents, and dialogue are drawn from the authors' imaginations and are not to be construed as real. Any resemblance to actual events or persons, living or dead, is entirely coincidental.

MISSHITSU NO KAGI KASHIMASU
Copyright © 2002 by Tokuya Higashigawa
English translation rights arranged with Kobunsha Co., Ltd., Tokyo

Lending the Key to the Locked Room
English translation copyright © 2020 by John Pugmire

All rights reserved. No part of this book may be used or reproduced in any manner whatsoever without written permission except in the case of brief quotations embodied in critical articles and reviews.

For information, contact: pugmire1@yahoo.com

FIRST AMERICAN EDITION
Library of Congress Cataloguing-in-Publication Data
Higashigawa, Tokuya
[*MISSHITSU NO KAGI KASHIMASU* English]
MISSHITSU NO KAGI KASHIMASU / Tokuya Higashigawa
Translated from the Japanese by Ho-Ling Wong

Contents

PROLOGUE

I shall refrain from providing a map showing the exact location of the city. If you truly need to know, the best I can do is to tell you that it lies east of the Chiba Prefecture and west of the Shinagawa Prefecture.

It was once a thriving port town whose daily catch of squid ranked amongst the most impressive in the whole country.

According to folklore, the armies of squid which would approach the port several times a year were so massive, it would appear as if the sea level itself had risen. They would wave their tentacles to the fishermen, inviting them out to sea to catch them.

Anyone who came home with a grand haul could become rich overnight and find themselves living in a fancy manor on a hill with a fantastic view.

Those were the good old days, when the economy was still thriving.

But the good days did not last forever, and the city and its people have lost their brilliance.

The massive armies of squid have not visited the port once in the last twenty years.

With the dream of becoming a millionaire overnight now a thing of the past, it was only natural that the feverish enthusiasm which once characterised the city would fade as well.

The place has been transformed into a bedroom town for white-collar workers who spend their day in the metropolis, and labourers who work day and night in the industrial district.

But the squid were by no means the only means of livelihood. Right through the middle of the city runs a Class A river emptying into the Pacific Ocean. No one should underestimate its importance to the citizenry.

Once upon a time, the river transported the squid that had been caught to cities further inland. Ever since that time, the river has been the lifeline of the city, and the image of boats loaded with freight plying their trade has become its symbol .

To this day, the whole city relies completely on the river for water for domestic use, so its importance to the people here cannot be overestimated. Even though the river isn't as awe-inspiring anymore due to pollution, the people still think proudly of it.

Because the river was mainly used for transporting squid, the inhabitants started calling the river the Ika River, or Squid River. Nobody felt any shame associated with the name. In fact, most people felt quite attached to it.

It was therefore only natural that this area took the name Ikagawa-Chō, or Squid River Town.

Three years ago, due to its rapidly growing population, it became a municipality, and the inhabitants became divided about the name of the new city.

In the end, the side that wanted to respect the historical name won, and that is how Ikagawa-Chō, once a town, became a proper city.

And that is why it's now called Ikagawa City.

But it seldom makes the news now. And, although the Japanese name for the city, *Ikagawa-shi,* sounds awfully like the word *ikagawashī* or "dubious", it is really not that bad a place.

CHAPTER ONE: BEFORE IT HAPPENED

1

Until as recently as ten years ago, Ikagawa City did not even have its own college. Young people graduating from high school had to commute to colleges in metropolitan Tōkyō, or actually move there to live.

The seventy-year-old mayor, who had been in office for four terms—a total of sixteen years—feared that, at that rate, the city would eventually be drained of its youth. Realising that the future of the city was in danger, he initiated an urgent project to create a college in Ikagawa City.

There were those who said that, if he were truly afraid the city was losing its youthful life-force, he should lead by example and retire at once, but the mayor decided to hang on for one more term to ensure Ikagawa City would get its college.

Its name: Ikagawa City College.

It had a number of faculties, including Law, Economics, and Literature, but the lack of a science faculty meant that it could not call itself a university.

Although the college was not ranked particularly highly, its presence nevertheless gave a boost to the city.

The centrepiece of the college, which attracted attention from all over Japan, was the Film Department.

If you were going to create a new college, why not have a department other colleges did not possess? Such was the simple-minded, desperate idea that could easily have backfired, but which fortunately turned out to be a roaring success.

How simple-minded was it? Think of those film festivals in rural places that dared to have taglines like "There Are No Film Theatres Here But We Do Have A Film Festival!" The Ikagawa City College Film Department was basically what happened if you took that idea to its extreme. For there are indeed no film theatres in Ikagawa City. To get to the closest theatre, you need to take the train for several stops, then change to a private railway line for several more. Ikagawa City was not somewhere you would choose to live if you were a lover of films. It was therefore nothing short of a miracle that they created a film department there.

Nevertheless! However! Even so! Despite these circumstances, the film department became a hit. There were more applications than they could accept. That was true for the first year, the second year, and the year after that as well.

Some might call it a declining industry, some might not even consider it a proper industry, but films have a way of capturing the hearts and minds of young people and never letting go.

And, because a four-year college course focusing on films and film history was so rare, students came from faraway places like Kyūshū, all the way in the south, and Hokkaidō, in the north.

Many have graduated from the department since its inception and some of those students have become major figures in the world of visual media.

And, of course, many graduates ended up working in the film industry.

Among the alumni is a young directing maestro who shoots "dubious" films, but he himself insists it has nothing to do with the fact he studied in Ikagawa City.

Ryūhei Tomura, a student of the Ikagawa City College Film Department, dreamt of becoming a legendary director when he first entered college, a dream many of his fellow students shared.

Ryūhei was truly convinced he could become the next Ozu or Kurosawa and even had delusions about Oscars and Palmes d'Or. Yes, you could call him a true film buff, or cinema addict. After all, no normal person would feel any emotional connection to such an objective.

Time flew by, and Ryūhei became a third-year student.

Like every student, by this time he had come to recognise the limits of his own talent. But, whilst he did worry somewhat about his future, hoping he could at least find work that had to do with films, he made little effort to actually secure such a job. For the time being, he simply wanted to spend the remaining days of his college life the best, or at least the most enjoyable, way he could. That was how he lived from day to day.

The one fact he had learned from his years of college was that Oscars and Palmes d'Or were concepts from a completely different world, and would forever be out of his reach.

That his parents had to pay the college fee (which was definitely not cheap) just so that their son could learn that obvious lesson, made Ryūhei feel ashamed. So one evening, he called them, full of laudable intentions.

'I'm going to find a normal job. Film director is not for me,' he confessed honestly. But his mother, who sounded over the moon, answered: 'So you finally came to your senses. Wonderful. It's a good thing we sent you to college.'

That was when things fell into place in Ryūhei's mind. He had gone to college to chase his dream, but his parents had let him go so as to force him to give it up. The hand holding the receiver trembled as Ryūhei was overcome with feelings of gratitude. Could you believe his parents!

Flushed with emotion, he replaced the receiver and started thinking about what to do next.

He didn't like the idea of just giving up completely. He knew he would have to find a normal job, just like everyone else, of course. But at the very least, he wanted to find something that had to with the media, visual media preferably.

Despite their popularity, the size of film and television productions is actually smaller than people think, and there are usually few openings. Most students believed that, to get one of those positions, you either needed to have some award or fantastic portfolio to show off your talent, or have very impressive connections.

And Ryūhei did indeed have connections to one particular company.

It was a small film production company that was a subsidiary of the local television station IKA. The name of the company was, not surprisingly, the IKA Film Company.

Ryūhei liked the fact that it actually called itself Film Company. It wasn't just a name, though: the IKA Film Company did indeed produce films.

However, they did not work on the kind of film that would show in normal theatres, where an adult would pay 1,800 yen for a regular ticket. The company produced specialised films, such as documentaries or educational films. No dazzling blockbusters there.

If successful, it would mean him landing a film-related job right here at home, so the idea of working there was very alluring.

Ryūhei's ally in his quest to secure a job at IKA Film Company was Kōsaku Moro, who worked in the General Affairs Department there.

Kōsaku Moro was twenty-five years old, three years senior to Ryūhei. The two had become acquainted two years earlier, when

Moro was a fourth-year student at the Ikagawa City College Film Department, and was working on a documentary as his graduation project. First-year student Ryūhei was also involved with the production. Can the reader guess in what capacity?

In the credits it said: Assistant-Director & Lighting Assistant & Filming Assistant & Timekeeper.

This title said it all. People who worked on Moro's project still tell tales of Ryūhei's incomparable exploits during the recording.

If Ryūhei gladly did all those chores back then, it was only because he was still a green first-year student. By the time he became a third-year, he realised he had no intention of ever working that hard again. But Moro still thought of Ryūhei as the person who worked himself to the bone for his graduation project, so he still looked after Ryūhei, even after he graduated.

They would have drinks together, or he would give Ryūhei advice about his graduation project, or show him rare films he had managed to find. Ryūhei would also visit Moro in his flat to watch videos and talk about films, and often ended up spending the whole night there.

Ryūhei hoped to make use of the connection to get a job.

Ryūhei was open to Moro about his hopes of landing a job at the company. At first, Moro was not quite convinced about how serious Ryūhei was, but he eventually came to realise how committed the student was, and promised to see what he could do. This happened in the autumn of Ryūhei's third year.

Although students naturally try to secure a job as soon as possible after graduation, Ryūhei was secretly a little worried as to whether he might have played his card too early but, to his surprise, his timing turned out to have been perfect. A new year started and, near the end of January, Moro gave Ryūhei a call.

'Hey, Tomura? It's been a while. Is your graduation project going well?'

'Yes, it's slow but steady.'

Ryūhei was going to make an experimental film with his friends. His title this time was "Director & Lighting & Filming & Timekeeper".

Basically, it was the same title he had as a first-year student, *sans* the "assistant" part. The film was planned to be unprecedented, one of a kind, astonishing and completely crazy.

'Slow, eh? Well, just keep at it, you still have more than a year before graduation. And speaking of graduation, how are your credits? If you don't plan them out now, you won't make it in your final year.'

'Oh, no problems there.'

At Ikagawa City College, courses were graded as S, A, B, C, D and Failed. The number of courses Ryūhei had passed with an A or higher could be counted on one hand but, at any rate, he didn't have to worry about not having enough credits to graduate.

'Aha. So your final year should be easy. The graduation project shouldn't pose any problems either, as long as you do what's expected. Great, great.'

'My only worry now is just getting a job.'

'Oh, you don't need to fret about that. I talked with my boss about you, and he said he'd leave it up to me. So I'd say you're fine now.'

'Eh? Do—does that mean, I've got…'

Ryūhei felt his mind about to explode. To be exact, the expectation of one particular word had instantly filled his whole mind. It was the magic word which every student looking for a job wanted whispered sweetly in their ear.

Ryūhei desperately wanted to hear that word spoken out loud.

His wish apparently made it across the telephone line, because Moro didn't hesitate to say the word.

'Consider yourself in possession of a *naitei*. You're going to be hired once you've graduated.'

A *naitei* is the informal promise of a company that they will employ a person after graduation, and is the one thing all students in Japan dream of, starting their third year in college.

'Really! You're going to hire me!'

'Well, it's still early, so consider it a pre-*naitei*.'

Ryūhei regretted asking again. Now his *naitei* had just got demoted one rank.

'A pre-*naitei*, or even a pre-pre-*naitei*, I love them all! Thank you so much!'

Ryūhei was so excited he started bowing to the telephone with the receiver in his hand. It looked a bit silly, but at that time Ryūhei was so happy, he would even have bowed to a three-year-old child.

Ryūhei had not expected it would go so smoothly. At a time when it was difficult to find employment, Ryūhei had expected that it might take more than a year to find something. But now he had a *naitei* in his pocket with almost no effort! His incredible luck even scared him for a second.

Ryūhei thanked the heavens. Thanked the kind Moro. And he thanked his past self, who, as a first-year student, did every chore on set with a stupid smile on his face. This was of course the first time in his life that he did something as curious as expressing gratitude to himself.

2

The following day, Ryūhei announced to everyone he met at college that he had found employment. Most of his friends gave the usual reaction, such as "Congratulations!" or "I'm so jealous!" but there were also a few rude persons who asked out loud why in heaven's name he would choose IKA Film Company.

They couldn't understand why Ryūhei's first choice was this small company, and why he hadn't tried with one of the major companies first. Ignoring these opinions was of course the best course of action, but there was one person's opinion Ryūhei couldn't just ignore.

Her name was Yuki Konno.

At the time, Yuki was Ryūhei's girlfriend. They had not seriously discussed their future yet, but their relationship was definitely not just a temporary thing. Ryūhei had always assumed they'd keep on dating even after they had graduated and become members of the workforce. Their relationship was that serious.

But the moment she heard the rumours about Ryūhei landing a job, she went to see him to give him an explosive message.

'Let's break up.'

There was no warning timer on the bomb, and Ryūhei's heart was shattered on the spot.

It happened right at noon, during the break. Location: a corner in the college cafeteria. As may be imagined, it was very crowded there, hardly the place to break up.

'Wa—wait, let's talk this over! We can work something out!'

Flabbergasted, Ryūhei shouted a line that could have been spoken by a president who was about to be killed by an assassin. But even Ryūhei didn't know what it was they had to talk about. Why did Yuki suddenly say she wanted to break up?

'I misjudged you,' Yuki started to explain. 'I thought you were meant for something bigger. You have the talent... actually, I wouldn't even mind if you didn't have the talent. But at the very least, I never expected you'd ready to give up so easily. Can you understand how disappointed I am in you? Why would you go to work there of all places!?'

'There? You mean IKA Film Company?'

14

'Yes! Why would you choose such a miserable place? Don't you even have the courage to go to Tōkyō and see what you could make of yourself there?'

There was nothing Ryūhei could say. To be honest, he really didn't have the courage. But do women nowadays still think you need to go to Tōkyō to be successful?

'What's the difference between Tōkyō and Ikagawa City?'

'Everything!' Her voice became louder by the second. It almost became scary. 'Do you really think there's a future to be had here?'

'Of course.'

'So you have a future here. Okay. But not for me. I can't imagine my future in this squid-stinking city.'

Ryūhei had never thought of this place as reeking of squid. He tried to convince Yuki.

'It's important to have dreams, but you also need to make a living, so…'

'Keep those pragmatic stories to yourself, I don't need to hear them.'

Ryūhei crossed his arms as he looked at Yuki with a heavy heart.

If she didn't want to listen to reality, did she want to hear him tell some fairy tale?

Perhaps he should do an imitation of Orson Welles and talk about the invasion of Martians. Or should he tell her about how he made it to Hollywood, bought a manor in Beverly Hills and danced with Gloria Swanson on Sunset Boulevard?

No, it wasn't necessary anymore. Yuki had lost her calm. She had expected too much from Ryūhei and now felt betrayed by him. Could he blame her?

'You're the worst. A coward. A liar. A chicken. A weakling!'

Ryūhei was only looking at her fast-moving mouth. Just let her say whatever is on her mind now.

'Stupid stupid stupid!'

By now she had regressed to a kid in elementary school. She had probably exhausted all the negative language she knew. Perhaps she would use language from children's books now.

Ryūhei actually became curious as to what she would say next.

'Stupid, pervert, bad-in-bed!'

That was one thing he couldn't let slide! Ryūhei, too, opened his mouth.

'Bad-in-bed? Tha—that has nothing to do with this!'

'Oh, well, I'm truly sorry,' Yuki first pretended to apologise. 'But it has everything to do with this. It's more important than you think.'

And that was the second bomb she threw.

There was nothing he could say any more. The white flag went up.

And that was the story of how Ryūhei was promised a job, in exchange for his girlfriend.

After a while, rumours went around campus that "Ryūhei Tomura was so bad at it that his girlfriend dumped him." Part of their fight in the cafeteria had gone off to live its own life. The way rumours can evolve into their own truths is truly frightening.

All Ryūhei could do was tell himself that nothing could be done about it now. Yuki could go find a guy with grand dreams and they'd live a thrilling life which would make her forget about the real world. He would go to work, with both feet planted firmly on the ground. That was all there was to it.

Their break-up had been so explosive, Ryūhei's feelings for Yuki Konno cooled off almost instantly. He didn't regret splitting up. It was the best choice for both of them, he decided.

3

However, Ryūhei's feelings did explode unexpectedly. It happened about ten days after their break-up, halfway through February.

Ryūhei had gone out drinking with five to eight friends (he didn't quite remember) and after quite a lot of gin and *shōchū* (he didn't quite remember), he raised his voice and started a rumpus in the bar, even starting a fight with a drunken white-collar worker outside before he returned home. He had been mainly on the receiving end. (He didn't remember anything of the fight.)

When he woke up the following morning, he found he had miraculously made it back to the entrance hall of his flat. He couldn't remember whether he had made it home on his own, or whether someone had helped him. But he suspected the latter.

Because every single bone in his body hurt and he couldn't even stand up straight. It took him a while before he managed to get up and, as he washed his face, the pain made him grimace.

The area around his eyebrows hurt. And the skin there felt rough.

Worried, he looked at his own face in the mirror. There was a dark bulge right between his eyebrows. He had been bleeding there, but by now the blood had already dried and hardened.

Ryūhei had numerous minor wounds on his cheeks and forehead, all dirty with sand.

His face looked so absolutely awful, he even felt sorry for himself.

Ryūhei suddenly felt concerned. Had he got into some trouble last night? Anxiously, he decided to call his good friend Yūji Makita.

'Give it to me, what awful misfortunes befell me last night?'

Yūji Makita's explanation came instantly.

'You started a brawl with some company worker you didn't even know. Don't you remember a thing? You're unbelievable.'

According to Yūji, the man Ryūhei fought had been extremely agile and packed a heavy punch. Perhaps he had been a boxer in a previous life.

'Aha,' Ryūhei nodded while holding the receiver to his ear. 'So I don't remember a thing because of the flurry of heavy punches that hit me.'

'No,' his friend immediately contradicted him. 'That's probably the booze. You decided to drink like a madman yesterday. Don't go blaming others for that.'

'…Oh.'

He guessed that it was probably his own fault.

'By the way, as you ran towards the guy, you cried out her name, you know.'

'Whose name?'

'Yuki Konno. You looked like the devil as you screamed "Yukiiii" and jumped at the man. Your opponent actually looked scared at that moment.'

And still Ryūhei couldn't recall any of it. But he could imagine the scene. It was probably true that it happened.

'And then you started hugging the sign with the time schedule at the bus stop. "Yukiiiii, you damn hussy, I'm going to kill yaaaa!" you were yelling.'

'…'

No way. That couldn't be true. Ryūhei couldn't believe it.

'And in the taxi, you started clinging to the driver and…'

'Okay, okay, I got it. Heard all I wanted to hear.'

He had heard enough to feed his self-loathing.

On the surface, Ryūhei seemed to be indifferent to his break-up with Yuki, but the cold truth was that he had been unable to let it go.

Ryūhei spent the following days sulking.

It was Kōsaku Moro who tried to get him out of his blue mood. Ryūhei received a call from Moro in the last week of February.

'Not feeling so good? You need to move on. How about coming around to my place next week? Perhaps there's a film you want to see? Tell me. We can watch it together.'

17

'Thank you. I can think of one film then....'

Ryūhei named the title of a minor film called *Massacre Manor*. They would meet in a week, on the twenty-eighth of February.

CHAPTER TWO: THE FIRST DAY

1

Let's start right away with the events that occurred on the first day of the incident. However, before we start, there is something that needs to be explained. That is the matter regarding the perspective used in this story.

It is common when narrating how an incident occurred, to use the perspective of the victim, the culprit, or perhaps a witness. It is the usual technique employed in mystery fiction. However, in order to grasp the whole outline of an actual case, one also has to accept the fact that one single perspective will not be able to cover all the pertinent facts.

It should be obvious by now that the incident told in this novel will revolve around Ryūhei Tomura. And this novel will mainly follow the events through his eyes. However, that will not be sufficient.

To address this insufficiency, one more narrative perspective will be presented at this point.

To put it simply, it's the point of view of the police.

The technique of using two different points of view to portray a case is not particularly unusual. Actually, it's quite common. Some readers might be put on their guard, suspecting that having two distinct perspectives will provide room for some kind of deception aimed at the reader, but this is not that kind of story. The purpose of this dual structure is to allow the reader to jump between the two perspectives, allowing them to have a complete view of how the case develops.

Well then, you might ask: who is this person who can freely switch between the perspectives of both Ryūhei Tomura and the police? Yes, I can hear you asking that exact question.

There are several possible answers to that question. You can think of me as that Higashigawa guy whose name is on the cover of this book. Or you can think of me as one of the characters of this tale. Or you can consider me the omniscient narrator, who is often seen in mystery fiction. Some refer to it as "the point of view of God", but Japanese readers might not be familiar with this term. Perhaps it's due to the large number of atheists in Japan.

Anyway, the narrative perspective will constantly change in this story. In a film, this would be called a crosscut. Some readers might find this a bit perplexing, so allow me to apologise now.

But this is the reason why a duo of police detectives will appear at this point. And please note that they are not the culprits. In classical mystery fiction, police detectives often have to play a clown's role, so we can at least pay courtesy to them by not making them murderers as well.

It shouldn't come as a surprise that the Ikagawa City Police Station is located within Ikagawa City. The three-storied building of reinforced concrete is located along the canal, slightly removed from the city centre. Even though it should be an intimidating place, the building is actually in pretty bad shape due to years and years of erosion from the sea breeze.

Plans to reconstruct the building had been proposed several times, and disappeared as often. Currently, "an eye was being kept on the state of the building".

Even from far away, it was clear that the walls, which were once pure white, had faded to a dirty grey colour. Going back to the original white was impossible now, no matter how much you polished the walls.

If you come closer and put your face to one of the walls, it's possible to make out the countless number of cracks with your bare eyes, almost like worms crawling around. Many of the people working here know about the cracks, but seeing as nobody speaks about them, you can assume nothing is being done.

And if you approach the building even closer and rub your nose against the wall, you'll probably be identified as a highly suspicious character and be questioned by the police. So don't do it. There are cops everywhere there.

Now imagine a middle-aged man standing behind the police station, silently smoking a cigarette as he stares at the water surface of the canal. His stern face and well-built body make him look like a labourer. One of those tanned labourers who work up a sweat beneath the blazing sun. But this man is not a worker on one of the squid fishing boats.

He is none other than Chief Inspector Sunagawa, without whom, it was said, the Ikagawa City Police Station would not be the same. Hobbies: Questioning people. Not married, no children. No debts. No criminal record. (What a guy!)

Before I explain why Chief Inspector Sunagawa was staring at the canal, allow me to introduce one more character: Detective Shiki, the subordinate of Chief Inspector Sunagawa. Shiki appeared from one corner of the building and when he spotted the chief inspector standing near the canal, he ran up to his boss.

'Chief Inspector, are you killing time here again!?'

'Oh, it's you, Shiki.' The Chief Inspector reacted calmly, without moving his eyes away from the canal. 'I'm not killing time, as you put it. This is part of my daily routine. I can't skip this part.'

'What are you looking at? Is there a body floating in the water?'

'Of course not. If there had been a body, everyone here would be overjoyed, err, I mean, there'd be a great commotion. But look, here's one, here's another, and over there as well.'

Shiki squinted his eyes and tried to find whatever the chief inspector was pointing at. But he didn't see anything at all. Wait, he did see something floating in the water, almost like polka dots on the surface.

'What's that? It's almost like... gelatine.'

'Stupid, those are jellyfish! Here's one, two, three. There are many of them today.'

'A—and what about them?'

'Whenever a bunch of jellyfish appears in this canal, you can expect rain in a few hours. That is what many years of experience have taught me. You can believe in that rule.'

'So you were predicting the weather?'

Indeed, Chief Inspector Sunagawa's special talent was to predict the weather. A special talent not really worth boasting about.

'And what's wrong with that? I'm pretty accurate.'

'I wasn't talking about your accuracy. You're a police detective, not a weather forecaster.'

'And what business brings you to me, a police detective? Just tell me now, I'm busy.'

'Didn't look that way. Ahem.' Shiki looked away from the water. 'I've got something better than the weather. It's an emergency. Well, it's just a bunch of sailors fighting. Shall we go?'

'I don't want to go.'

'It's more fitting work for a detective than predicting the weather with the help of jellyfish. Come on.'

Shiki had to drag Chief Inspector Sunagawa away from the canal. Soon a siren rang. The number of jellyfish in the canal kept on increasing even after their observer had left. More and more came. If

Chief Inspector Sunagawa's experience was correct, Ikagawa City would be due for a major rainfall that evening.

2

The evening of Wednesday, the twenty-eighth of February was even chillier than usual.

The blanket of freezing, heavy air almost froze the whole city and was accompanied by gusts coming from the sea. The winters in Ikagawa City are always bitter, but the cold season had been particularly severe this year. There was not a hint of spring, even though the calendar had almost turned to March. Nobody doubted that tonight, the temperature would again almost reach freezing point.

As they had agreed the week before, Ryūhei visited the flat of Kōsaku Moro that evening.

It's a fifteen-minute walk from the centre of Ikagawa City, and as you reach the riverside you turn left, walk another five minutes alongside the riverside bicycle path in the direction of the sea, and when you reach Saiwaichō Park there, you go to the neighbouring area, where… To those not familiar with the lay of the land of Ikagawa City, this explanation probably sounds exactly as informative as a life insurance contract.

In fact, the complicated geographical features of the neighbourhood are not particularly important for this tale.

The reader only needs to remember that Moro's flat is located next to Saiwaichō Park.

It's a broken-down two-storey building made of reinforced concrete. Its inhabitants might think it rude to describe their home as broken-down, but that's the truth.

The dreary-looking concrete box had been built over twenty years ago and was well on its way to becoming a ruin.

The owner, too, was probably just waiting until the building fell apart on its own, and only performed the most basic of repairs. The whole place looked very shabby.

And yet the name of this apartment building was White Wave Apartments. A building might age but its name doesn't, which resulted in the contrast. The person who gave the building its name had probably not thought that far ahead.

Ryūhei passed through Saiwaichō Park and entered the grounds of White Wave Apartments. Beyond the little entrance gate, which had probably been white once, were four doors. Moro's flat was the one closest to the entrance gate, Flat 4.

Ryūhei looked at his watch as he weighed his options. 'It's rude to arrive too early, but it's even ruder to arrive late…'

They were going to meet at seven. His wristwatch was showing ten to seven.

'But if I arrive on the dot, it'll look as if I timed it exactly.'

Ryūhei stood there in front of Flat 4 on the ground floor as he pondered what to do next. There was no name plate next to the door, but he had visited this place so often, there was no way he could be mistaken about the flat.

There were rust stains here and there on the metal door. Each time Ryūhei visited this place, he automatically thought of the door of the gymnasium storage at his middle school. One look was enough to tell him this was a sturdy door.

There was one major advantage to this apartment building that needs mentioning.

Because the building was already in such bad shape, you were allowed to modify your rooms the way you wanted. Obviously, you weren't allowed to let the building collapse on itself, but all things considered, a lot was allowed.

Moro's flat consisted of two rooms and a kitchen. But what would be mere fantasy for a lowly white-collar worker, Moro had made a reality. He had one of his rooms made completely soundproof, set a screen on one of the walls and had placed a projector, large speakers, an amplifier and a subwoofer for the low tones in the room to create his own private home theatre.

The whole makeover cost at least a million yen. So let it be clear that Moro hadn't move into the building because he was badly off. He had chosen this place because he could freely refurbish the rooms. He was a person with a strong will.

You could say that Ryūhei felt respect for Moro exactly because of his character. Ryūhei had watched films in Moro's home theatre several times now. Each time he visited, he dreamt of having such a place of his own one day. That was why he needed to find a good job. And for that, he needed to stay in Moro's good books. It was his most important mission.

With this clear objective in mind, Ryūhei rang the bell of Flat 4. It didn't take long for the familiar face of Kōsaku Moro to appear at the door.

He had a rather self-composed air about him, despite being only twenty-five. The outline of his face was heart-shaped, and it was topped by some stiff hair. His narrow eyes with admirable sight added to the open nature of his character. He had a moderate hooknose, which always reacted to spring pollen. He had thin lips, surrounded by some pale spots where he shaved. He had rather thick hair, and when he was in college, he was actually known for his beard which rivalled Spielberg's. But for the readers who have never seen Moro, this detail will seem as meaningless a parade of words as the clauses in a car insurance contract. If only I could just show you a photograph of him.

Anyway, he was neither handsome nor unattractive. Just imagine the kind of ordinary twenty-five- year -old man you see everywhere.

'Oh, you're here. Come inside.'

Moro was dressed in a pair of brown pants and a thin sweater, with a grey fleece jacket. He usually dressed in such a rough, plain manner. He let Ryūhei inside the entrance hall. Moro's coat was hanging from a hook on the wall to the right. It, too, was a plain black colour.

'Thank you.'

The entrance hall led to a small corridor. Two of the doors in the corridor led to the bathroom and the toilet. Not a prefabricated bathroom with a built-in toilet, as most flats have. Moro's had a separate bathroom and toilet. There was a small kitchen to the right of the corridor, and two more doors at the end. One led to the living room and the other to Moro's beloved home theatre.

Ryūhei was first taken to the living room, which was comfortably warm because of a heater there. Ryūhei could feel his body finally relax after walking in the cold outside.

'Bet it's cold outside.'

'Yeah, it is rather chilly.'

'But I think it's going to rain tomorrow.' Moro did the usual weather talk as he started clearing the newspapers and magazines from the table. 'Sit down, I'll make some tea.'

'Oh, you shouldn't,' replied Ryūhei, in the customary manner. But Moro was quick, as if he had already prepared everything, and it didn't take long for him to bring steaming cups of *genmaicha*, green tea with roasted brown rice.

Soon the chat turned naturally to the topic of work.

'I think you may be labouring under a misunderstanding,' Moro began, as he squinted his narrow eyes. 'Were you under the impression that my place is really popular, and that it's hard to land a job there?'

'It's not?'

'Not at all,' replied Moro, shaking his head. 'To be honest, we're always shorthanded. Filmmaking might sound good on paper, but in the end, we're just a small subcontractor. Still, it's a specialist business, so people have to work pretty hard. Lots of people end up quitting.'

'O—oh.'

Ryūhei could feel his heart jump.

'Yeah. I wouldn't say we'd hire anyone, but it's not that hard to find employment at my place. It's what happens after you get in.'

'That doesn't sound very reassuring.'

'Well, you don't have to worry too much about it. It's still more than a year before you'll be hired.'

'So you mean I should study and get prepared now?'

'No, I mean you should make sure you have all the fun you can have now before you start working.'

'Oh.'

'Everyone always has to work overtime,' said Moro as he sipped from his tea. He seemed to like his own home brew a lot. 'It's day after day of overtime. You'd think we'd be violating the Labour Standards Act somehow. So yeah, enjoy your free time while you can. Or you'll regret it later.'

'…'

Ryūhei didn't know how to react to this advice. Or was it a veiled warning? Well, at least Moro was being honest with him, Ryūhei thought, as his shoulders drooped.

'Hahaha, you don't need to be that disappointed. It's not that awful, of course. But if you ever need my help, I'll be there for you. Unless it's about money problems. But I have to say, you're a mighty curious character to have chosen my place. You've got spirit, that much I can say.'

'Huh.'

No wonder it had been so easy to get employed there. But at least it was better than not getting employed, Ryūhei thought, looking on the bright side.

After all the talk about work, Ryūhei and Moro started their film buff chat.

'By the way, I want to see the video. Is it in your day bag?'

'The video?'

For a second, Ryūhei was surprised by Moro's question.

'The video you talked about on the phone, the one you wanted to see. I think the title was *Murder Wood,* or something like that?'

Murder Wood was the local title of *The Conformist,* an early work by the famous Italian film director Bernardo Bertolucci, but it was not the film Ryūhei wanted to watch.

'Not *Murder Wood.* It's *Massacre Manor.* And of course I have it with me.'

Ryūhei took out a video tape from his bag.

Massacre Manor was director Ryūtarō Kawauchi's ambitious mystery film. But Ryūtarō Kawauchi was not a famous film director, and few people knew of its existence. To put it bluntly, the film was not a masterpiece, nor had it been made by a well-known director.

When Ryūhei was asked the week before whether there was a film he wanted to see, the title had popped into his head immediately. Moro seemed unfamiliar with it, but didn't seem to mind. They agreed that Ryūhei would get the tape from the video rental shop and that they'd watch it together in Moro's home theatre.

Ryūhei had picked the tape up from the store today on his way over.

Incidentally, the name of the clerk at the video rental shop was Kazuki Kuwata, one of Ryūhei's classmates and a self-proclaimed film buff as well. This is what he had to say when he saw Ryūhei was going to rent *Massacre Manor:* 'Just don't. It's a waste of money. And a waste of time. I'm not lying. I've been working here for six months you know, and you're the first one to ever rent that video. Curiosity *will* kill the cat in this case!'

Kuwata had rather strong opinions about the film.

But one should not pay attention to anyone who tries to impose their own subjective opinions on the mind of a customer who is about to see a film. It's completely against the film buff rules of etiquette.

Which is why Ryūhei felt even more compelled to watch the film that night.

'Is it long?' Moro wanted to know the length.

'It's a bit on the long side. It says two hours and thirty minutes on the label here.'

Ryūhei passed the tape to Moro. He looked at the label himself. It had indeed a runtime of two hours and thirty minutes. It also said Kantō Film Corporation, 1977.

'1977? I have a bad feeling about this,' Moro mumbled.

Ryūhei had a hunch where that feeling came from. As a film buff, he had some knowledge about the history of mystery films.

The great mystery film boom of Japanese cinema occurred in the latter half of the seventies.

Some say it all started with the film adaptations of *Inspector Imanishi Investigates* or *The Inugami Curse*, but it could also be said the source had been *The Honjin Murders*, the film that saved the independent film agency ATG.

At any rate, those were incredible times, with many hit adaptations of works by Seichō Matsumoto and Seishi Yokomizo.

But whenever there's a boom, you also have people who try to jump on the bandwagon. That was true for the mystery film boom as well.

Following countless films that were trying to piggyback on the success, the boom eventually died out. Kantō Film Corporation's 1977 film *Massacre Manor* was produced in the middle of that period.

Ryūhei had to admit alarm bells were ringing.

But still, he wanted to watch the film. If it was truly that awful a film, well, at least he'd have something to talk about.

'It's probably like one of those mockbusters. Can't say I have high expectations.'

Moro seemed to have lost interest before it had even started, so Ryūhei quickly tried to get on his good side again.

'Don't judge the film too fast! Isn't that exactly why we were going to watch it ourselves, to see if it's just a mockbuster, or perhaps a hidden gem?'

'Of course I'm going to watch it…' Moro started, but then seemed to recall something. 'But how about taking a bath first? I bet you always need to go to the public bathhouse? How about having a proper bath once in a while? We can start the film after you're done.'

'Oh, well, if you insist.'

Moro didn't need to insist. Poor Ryūhei lived in a flat without its own bathroom and by now it had become customary for Ryūhei to use Moro's bathroom whenever he visited.

Starving students all across the world would probably do the same as Ryūhei, in order to save the fee for the public bath.

Moro, too, had grown accustomed to this ritual and never failed to offer Ryūhei a warm bath. Ryūhei accepting the offer with delight was part of the ceremony as well.

Ryūhei took his bath. There is no need to detail the fifteen minutes he spent in the bathtub there.

3

And whilst Ryūhei is soaking in the bath, we shall make use of the time to see what those two detectives are up to. Funnily enough, they too were having a little happening with a bath.

Having received the report on the brawl between the sailors, Chief Inspector Sunagawa and Shiki made their way to the wharf, but by the time the duo arrived there, the small fight had transformed into a melee between the sailors and police officers. Sailors who were trying to cover for each other, and police officers who had gone all the way to answer the call and weren't going back empty-handed. This happened surprisingly often in the city.

In the end, the people involved in the first fight and the underlying cause were all forgotten in the chaos. One man who pushed an officer into the sea was arrested for obstruction and that was it. After dispatching all those involved, all they had to show for it was one arrest and one wet officer.

'See, that's why I said I didn't want to come. Good grief, what a waste of time,' Chief Inspector Sunagawa grumbled. Meanwhile, cold sea water was leaking from Shiki's clothes.

'Yo-yo-you're right si-si-sir, we-we-we shouldn't have come…'

Chief Inspector Sunagawa stared in surprise at his subordinate. 'Shiki, what happened to you?'

'Uuugh, I was pushed into the sea…'

'That sole victim was you!?' Sunagawa looked at Shiki with pity. 'The water must be cold in the winter. (Of course it was.) But you must be some kind of superman, to have made it back to shore on your own.'

'No-no-nobody came to help me…' whimpered Shiki as he trembled.

'You just don't stand out. But we got our man, so all's well that ends well.'

'Nothing is well!' barked Shiki with his eyes wide open.

'Okay, okay.' Even Sunagawa was taken aback by Shiki's extraordinary appearance and attitude. 'I get it, so, ah, how about a bath? There's a sauna in front of the train station. I'll drive.'

'Please! Get me to a bath before I dieeeeee,' cried Shiki with his (almost) dying breath.

And so Chief Inspector Sunagawa had Shiki sit down in the passenger's seat in their unmarked police car. What did the people think when they saw a police car with the sirens on speeding through the city and parking right in front of the sauna?

Anyway, Shiki was brought to a sauna room moments before he froze to death and was finally unfrozen there. Experiencing how a piece of frozen meat must feel in the microwave may be rare, but not something Shiki could appreciate.

'It's so good to be aliiiive.' Shiki did gain a renewed respect for his life.

Once the pallor of his skin had faded, Shiki got out, which led to a new problem: what was he going to wear? He couldn't wear his brine-soaked coat. Naturally, he didn't carry a spare set of clothes with him either. Seeing Shiki in trouble in the locker room, Chief Inspector Sunagawa thought of something.

'Leave it up to me,' Sunagawa said as he beat his own chest. 'I know someone who works here. He can probably lend you something. Wait a second.'

Sunagawa left Shiki alone in the locker room. Sunagawa returned a while later, holding a paper bag in his hands. Its contents were, indeed, clothes.

A pair of leather pants with a studded belt. A red shirt and a dark jacket with an embroidered dragon. Once he got dressed, Shiki looked like nothing more than a low-ranking mob member.

'It suits you,' said Sunagawa thoughtlessly.

Shiki, however, was not very happy. 'Sir, your friend, what kind of person is he? Is he a member of the *yakuza*?'

'Of course not! He's just someone I've been keeping an eye on. When he was young he belonged to a motorcycle gang. But now he's reformed and working here.'

'He may be reformed, but his fashion sense is still the same,' Shiki sighed as he took a good look at the wild dragon in the mirror. How could a cop wear this? Even those "loose cannons" in cop dramas didn't dress like that.

'Stop complaining, at least you have something to wear now.' Chief Inspector Sunagawa crushed Shiki's salty coat into a ball. 'This can be disposed of, I assume? I'll throw it away.'

The coat was already in the dustbin before he had finished his sentence.

'Chief Inspector?'

'Yes?'

'That's my police ID you just threw away.'

'You fool! You should have told me earlier!'

Sunagawa quickly thrust his arm in the dustbin to retrieve the symbol of the police force.

4

Once he got out of the bath, Ryūhei was offered a maroon sweat suit by Moro, which he put on. Ryūhei was in the best of moods, being treated like a king. The tension he had felt earlier had disappeared completely now and he felt very relaxed, almost as if he were at home.

'Let's watch the film now,' he said, but Moro stopped him.

'Just a moment. I want to watch the sports news first. It won't take long.'

The seven o'clock public news broadcast showing on the small television in the living room was almost over. The short sports segment would be followed by the weather forecast.

'What kind of sports news? Soccer? Baseball?'

It was the end of February. Ryūhei couldn't think of any major sports events going on.

The news continued.

'And now for sports. The Baseball Pro League's exhibition games have started. The Hiroshima-Kintetsu match was held in Nichinan. Much was expected of the new Hiroshima additions, but they were slaugh-slaugh, excuse me, slaughtered.'

These were just exhibition matches. Ryūhei remembered they were about to start at about this time. Still, that newsreader was pretty awful. As was the text.

Ryūhei was surprised that Moro was interested in the game between Hiroshima and Kintetsu.

Neither the Hiroshima Carps nor the Kintetsu Buffalos had many fans in Ikagawa City. Perhaps Moro was keeping it a secret exactly because there were so few fellow fans around. But still, Ryūhei thought Moro's interest in the game was quite unexpected.

'And now for news on the Olympic Games,' the newsreader started, at which Moro stretched his body.

'Let's go watch your film then.'

He apparently had no interest in this year's Olympics. Guess he's a Carps fan. Or perhaps a Buffalos fan... No, it can't be!

Ryūhei himself was living with the secret that he was in fact a Hanshin Tigers fan. As an honourable fellow warrior, he therefore refrained from prying into Moro's loyalties.

The news about the Olympics was over in a moment, and a weather forecaster in a dark suit had suddenly appeared on screen.

'And now, the weather forecast. This low-pressure area is approaching the Kantō region. At dawn tomorrow, the Kantō region will see thunderstorms and heavy local rainfall in the morning.'

Moro switched the television off with the remote control before the weather forecast had ended. He then seemed to recall something.

'Ever hear of predicting the weather with jellyfish? It's supposed to be really accurate. Some sailors once told me about it. Anyway, let's go and watch the film.'

Ryūhei and Moro left the living room and went together to the home theatre in the next room. The walls of the ten square metre wide room had been covered with soundproof material, making it feel more like an eight square metre room. Miscellaneous AV equipment had been set up in the limited space.

The shelves on the walls held an enormous video collection.

In the centre of the room stood a two-seater sofa and a small table.

It was a wonderfully luxurious room, decorated especially to enjoy films.

That Moro's family was quite well off must have helped as well, but it was Moro's strong desire to have his own film theatre that had made the room a reality.

'It's a good thing technology keeps on advancing, but it's also a curse. We're entering the era of DVDs now. That's all fine and dandy, but it means my video tape collection will be outdated soon. And it's not as if I can just exchange all these video tapes for DVDs. I really don't know what to do with them. Anyway, have a seat.'

Moro stood in front of the screen and made a small bow. Ryūhei responded with a modest round of applause.

'The film will start now. Please switch off your mobile phone,' asked Moro in a polite, gentlemanly manner. Though that lasted only for one sentence. 'I warn you, switch that thing off. If I hear even one sound…'

'If you hear one sound…?'

'You'll be fined one thousand yen!' Moro said coldly, with a nonchalant expression on his face. 'Don't say I didn't warn you.'

'You sure are strict here. But don't worry, I don't even have a mobile phone.'

'Eh? Most people have one nowadays, don't they?'

'Oh, I never liked them. Makes you feel as if you're chained to them. You know.'

Setting the matter of whether he liked them or not aside, Ryūhei had of course often made use of a mobile phone when he was still dating Yuki Konno. But after he broke up with her, he also said farewell to his phone. It was a bit embarrassing, so he didn't like talking about it.

'Okay then, let's roll the film.'

Moro placed *Massacre Manor* in the VHS player. The video deck was located at the back wall, behind the sofa, so as to not obstruct the view on the screen. It didn't take a second for the projector to cast its light on the screen. The film started at exactly seven-thirty.

Moro switched off the lights and soon the darkness was dispelled by the revived colours recorded a quarter-of-a-century earlier. Ryūhei felt as if he really were in a film theatre and was instantly sucked into the world on the screen.

5

"Incident at Takano Apartments in Saiwaichō. A young woman has fallen from the building. Police cars in the vicinity are to go there immediately. I repeat. Incident at Takano Apartments in Saiwaichō...'

The incident occurred at nine forty-five.

The raspy voice from the police radio reverberated through the dark car and brought Chief Inspector Sunagawa suddenly back to life. Until then, he had been sitting silently in the passenger's seat.

'What? Saiwaichō!? But that's just around the corner,' he said agitatedly. He leant forward and fiddled with the radio with his right hand. 'Let's pretend we didn't hear it.'

His right index finger pressed a button and switched the radio off. It went silent, but who did not remain silent was Shiki, who was sitting in the driver's seat.

'Si—sir, what are you doing? It's an incident, an incident, sir! We can't pretend nothing happened!'

'You still want to go on working today? You just don't learn. This time somebody might throw you in a fire.'

'I won't bother with fights with sailors anymore.' Shiki had had more than enough of that for one day. 'But this case may be a big one.'

'It's probably just an accident, or perhaps a suicide leap. Leave minor cases like that up to the guys from Prefectural.'

'Si—sir, that's what the Prefectural Police say to us! We're the local police!'

'I don't want to work overtime on this cold night, and I don't feel like ogling a corpse either. I want to go home, switch on the heater and have a nice cup of hot sake.'

'No. Sir, I'm going to switch the sirens on.'

'You'll be annoying the people in the neighbourhood with that racket.'

'In the name of justice.'

'Suit yourself.'

Shiki had been waiting for that response.

'Allow me to suit myself, then.'

Loud sirens sounded throughout Ikagawa City. Pedestrians turned around wondering what had happened, and cars on the road pulled over in surprise.

Shiki was racing at full speed towards Saiwaichō.

Thanks to the noisy sirens, their patrol car arrived in front of Takano Apartments in almost no time. Time: nine forty-eight precisely. If they hadn't paused to argue, they would have even arrived a minute earlier.

Onlookers had already gathered on the street. Two patrol officers were working to preserve the scene by sealing the area off with police tape.

'We did it, Chief Inspector! We're the first to arrive! How lucky!'

'Nothing to be happy about. It's not as if we'll be rewarded. Aren't you a bit too eager to work? It's as if you were reinvigorated by the sea water. You must have a strange body.'

Shiki himself had to admit his boss wasn't completely wrong. But still, there was something about the unique atmosphere of the scene of an incident hat always managed to tickle Shiki's senses. He simply couldn't sit still.

The two detectives stepped out of the car. Shiki was delighted, Sunagawa was discouraged.

Other police cars were also making their way to the scene. They could hear the noise of several sirens overlapping each other from far away. In a few minutes, this neighbourhood would be swarming with police cars.

Sunagawa and Shiki weaved their way through the crowd of onlookers and approached the two patrol officers. It wasn't quite clear whether Sunagawa's nonchalantly raised hand was a salute or whether he was just stretching his arms, but the officers quickly returned a salute and raised the police tape for him.

Shiki tried to follow his boss, but was stopped by one of the officers.
'Sir, this area is closed off. Please leave.'

The tape was lowered right in front of Shiki, as if it were the arm of a crossing gate. Shiki was taken aback at this treatment, but then realised why it had occurred.

'Oh, I'm dressed like some gang member, but I'm a detective. Here.'

Shiki felt ashamed as he showed his police ID. The patrol officer opened his eyes wide as he scrutinised the ID. The officer didn't say a thing, but Shiki could read "I can't believe this" from the man's face.

'Oh, you can let him in,' Sunagawa finally said. 'Don't mind his clothes, err, he was doing undercover work just now.'

'Undercover!' The officer cried out in surprise. 'You mean, just like they do in those police dramas? A cop disguises himself and starts snooping around inside a criminal organisation. How thrilling, how cool! Aha, that's why you're dressed like a former biker gang member!'

Chief Inspector Sunagawa nodded. Shiki decided to not react at all. The fact he was indeed wearing the clothes of a former biker gang member made him feel embarrassed.

The suspicious look on the patrol officer's face had transformed into one of admiration towards Shiki.

'Thank you for your continued efforts!'

'I—it's nothing,' Shiki responded.

'So where did you go undercover? Organised crime? The Murakawa Group perhaps, or the Maruwa Society?'

Shiki decided to answer truthfully. 'I was under water.'

The body was lying on the side of the street. The officers had managed to arrange for a white sheet to cover the victim. Sunagawa looked up at the towering Takano Apartments against a backdrop of the dark night sky. It was like a titan watching the scene.

He looked at where the victim was lying.

'The crime scene investigators haven't arrived yet, so we'd better stay away from her for now. Let's have a chat with the person who made the report while we wait for them.'

'A chat? You mean questioning?' Shiki corrected his superior.

'Some prefer to call it that.' It was the same to Sunagawa either way. 'You, can you bring me the person who reported this?'

The patrol officer quickly returned with a middle-aged man, apparently an ordinary office worker. The man seemed rather unnerved by the event and spoke rapidly as he introduced himself.

'My name is KōtaroTakanashi, fifty-one years old. I'm the head of the labour section at a transport company.'

'Alright. Could you tell me how you came to find the victim? At what time did it happen?'

'I know the exact time. It was nine forty-two on my watch.'

'Aha. Please allow me a look.' Chief Inspector Sunagawa took the man's left arm and placed his own left arm next to it.

Two shiny wristwatches around two wrists. To be exact, only the expensive watch of the other man was shiny. The cheap digital watch of the inspector looked as though it could stop at any minute.

But the two clocks did indicate more or less the exact same time.

'One minute to ten. More or less on the dot.' OK

'No, it's exactly on the dot. Managing labour in a company means being strict about the time. That's the one iron rule. Your watch is fifteen seconds slow.'

KōtaroTakanashi seemed to pride himself on his watch, although it seemed to leave Sunagawa unimpressed.

'Okay. Now please be good enough to tell me what happened at nine forty-two?'

'Of course,' replied the other, and started speaking rapidly.

'I was walking alone in the street on my way back home. It happened as I passed in front of this building. Suddenly there was a loud noise. Something had fallen about five metres in front of me. Can you imagine how frightened I was? At first I thought someone had thrown a sand bag at me from one of the balconies above. But as I carefully stepped forward, I realised it was a young woman. I immediately thought it must have been a suicide leap. So I checked my watch. It was nine forty-two.'

'Hmmm,' Sunagawa mumbled in a curious manner. 'So you didn't only discover the victim, you were actually witness to her death. Doesn't happen often.'

'Yes, first time it's happened to me. I can still feel my heart thumping.'

'But don't worry. It won't happen again,' said Sunagawa in a soothing manner. 'At least, probably not.'

'Probably.'

Shiki was screaming internally. Of course it wouldn't happen again! No way anyone was going to experience this two or three times in one lifetime!

Shiki decided to ask a few pertinent questions before everything turned to useless chatter.

35

'Was the woman dead when you found her?'

'Yes. There was blood everywhere. No way she was still alive....'

'Do you know which floor she fell from?'

'No, I really have no clue. I only saw the moment she crashed onto the street.'

'Have you ever seen the woman before?'

'No, I don't know her.'

'Thank you.' Shiki was done with his questions and returned the initiative to Sunagawa. The chief inspector urged the man to continue with his story.

'So what happened after you witnessed this woman's last moment?'

'I knew I had to get the police first. There's a police box (1) just up ahead, so I thought it would be quicker to run over there, rather than call the emergency line.'

'Shiki, get me that young patrol officer. Let's see what he has to tell us.'

Shiki brought over the patrol officer, who had been busy with keeping the onlookers away.

'My name is Katō, sir. Nobuo Katō. Stationed at Saiwaichō Police Box.'

'Go on.'

The patrol officer had obviously hoped that the chief inspector would remember his name, but Sunagawa had no interest at all in the name of a mere patrolman. He just started firing questions. As the officer answered, they confirmed that KōtaroTakanashi had been telling the truth.

'Mr. Takanashi rushed into our police box at nine forty-three or forty-four. If the victim fell at nine forty-two, his arrival time is about what you'd expect, considering the distance between this place and the police box. Yes, there's nothing wrong there.'

'Sorry, but let me have a look first,' Sunagawa said as he repeated his earlier action. He put his arm next to that of the officer and compared the times on their wristwatches. The results were the same.

'Seven minutes past ten. More or less on the dot.'

'Sir, my clock is exactly on the dot. It's the latest model, and is correct down to the second.' The officer seemed to be proud of his watch too. 'Sir, I think your watch is fifteen seconds slow.'

'Err, o—okay.' Chief Inspector Sunagawa wasn't the kind of person to actually mind that his watch was fifteen seconds slow.

(1) a police station with only three or four officers

'Anyway, what did you do after Mr. Takanashi told you about the fall?'

'We raced to the scene, of course, to block the area off.'

'And then we arrived a few minutes later?'

'Exactly. That is how it happened.'

Sunagawa had more questions for the officer. 'Would you happen to have any ideas about the identity of the victim? You had a look at her face, right? And you're stationed in this area.'

'Yes, I had a look. Her face wasn't… errr, but I recognised the hair and her body build. I believe she lives on the third floor of Takano Apartments.'

'And who might this woman be?'

The officer straightened up and responded crisply:

'A student of Ikagawa City College. I believe her name is Yuki Konno.'

'A student, eh?'

Sunagawa glanced once more at the body on the road.

At that moment, the crime scene investigators and medical examiner arrived, so the body could finally be inspected.

'Okay, go back to your post.'

'Yes sir.' The officer saluted, and walked away, but after a few steps, he suddenly turned around and walked up to Shiki.

'Yes?' Shiki asked curiously.

'I'm a bit embarrassed to ask you,' the officer said as he looked for the right words. 'What did you mean earlier?'

'Huh?'

'You see, I've never heard of the Undawata Group. Perhaps I heard you wrong? Was it the Umiwa Group? Or the Kuzuwata Group? But I can't say I ever heard of them either. It really bugs me…'

'…'

Katō seemed to be fascinated by the idea of undercover investigations. Perhaps he was one of those young men who had become a cop as a result of watching police dramas. He had taken Shiki's joke rather seriously.

'Hey, listen, I…'

Shiki was about to explain everything to Katō, when someone suddenly appeared in his field of vision.

'But that's…!'

It was a familiar face, a classmate from Shiki's high school. It had been years since he had last seen the man, but he had not changed much. He was standing on the other side of the yellow police tape, amongst the mob of onlookers looking his way.

'But that's Moro. Kōsaku Moro!'

'Eh?' Patrol officer Katō looked surprised.

'I wasn't talking to you.'

Shiki wanted to call out discreetly to his old classmate. As he was a cop and on duty, he couldn't just go and chat with an old friend, but nobody would get upset with him if it were just a moment.

Just at that moment, Kōsaku Moro, on the other side of the tape, caught sight of Shiki.

'Huh?'

For some reason the expression on Kōsaku Moro's face suddenly hardened. It was an expression of surprise and fear. Moro broke the gaze and disappeared into the crowd of onlookers.

Shiki was taken aback by the reaction of his old friend. What had happened? Had he forgotten about him?

'What's the matter?' Katō asked with concern.

'Oh, no, it's nothing.' Shiki recovered quickly. 'I thought I saw someone I know in the crowd. But perhaps I was wrong.'

'Oooi,' Sunagawa cried out to Shiki from a distance. 'Shikiii, what are you doing there? We've been given the okay to investigate the scene!'

The body was dressed in a beige sweat shirt and a pair of tight pants. It was a casual outfit, but it did show off her proportions. It was hard to tell whether she had been attractive because her face had been severely damaged and was not pleasant to look at.

It was clear that she had fallen to her death. Shiki thought to himself that young women falling from buildings usually turn out to be suicides. Perhaps she had been dumped, or perhaps she had been feeling desperate about her future. Or had there been something else?

Many thoughts passed through Shiki's mind, but all of his assumptions were rejected by the medical examiner. The veteran pointed out an extremely important fact.

'The woman's estimated time of death is around nine forty-five. She probably fell from a considerable height onto the street. The bruises on her face and her whole body were probably from the impact.'

'And I assume that's also her cause of death?'

Sunagawa obviously didn't expect anything else.

'No. I can't say for sure,' replied the examiner, choosing his words carefully. 'Besides the exterior damage from the fall, I also came across what appears to be a stab wound in her back. I cannot tell which was the cause of death.'

Sunagawa gasped at this unexpected discovery.

'Doc, did you say she was stabbed? But how?'

'I am just telling you the facts. At the very least, it's very possible this isn't a suicide. You don't go around stabbing yourself in the back.'

'So… it's murder.'

'Determining that is your job. All I can say is that it is not normal for someone to be stabbed in the back and then thrown off a building.'

'And what about the murder weapon?'

'Probably a small knife. Something with a thin, very sharp blade.'

'But you are sure her time of death is around nine forty-five?'

'No doubt about that,' the doctor said with emphasis. 'The body is still fresh. I wouldn't be able to do this job if I weren't able to narrow it down to a period of only a few minutes.'

According to the witness KōtaroTakanashi, the victim had hit the street at nine forty-two. As the examiner had said, he was only a few minutes off. Shiki was quite impressed.

At this point in the investigation it was clear the woman had not simply died: she was indeed a "victim".

The next problem was determining her identity. She had no papers on her, and there was also nothing unique about her clothes. Patrol officer Katō had stated the victim's hairstyle and build reminded him of a woman called Yuki Konno, but was he correct?

The first thing to do was to call the caretaker of Takano Apartments and get them to have a look at the victim. The caretaker was elderly, but seemed quite convinced.

'Yes, she looks like Ms. Konno, Flat 403. Her hair, and I think I have seen these clothes before too. Yes, I'm afraid it's her.'

It turned out she was indeed Yuki Konno, a student at Ikagawa City College.

Sunagawa and Shiki quickly went up to her flat. They got off at the third floor and stood in front of the door of Flat 403. The door had not been locked. The room was warm and the lights were still on, but there was no sign of anyone inside. They called out, but there was only silence as answer.

Sunagawa stepped inside first, followed by Shiki.

There was nothing amiss in the room itself. The television, the radio, the table and chairs, the bed with the striped-pattern cover: everything was neatly in place. But it did feel creepy how the oil fan heater was keeping an empty room warm. The room didn't have the cool air you'd expect from a murder scene. There was only a serene, yet lonely atmosphere in the room.

There was only one stain distinguishable on the moss green carpet.

'Hey, Shiki, look here.'

'But that's— !'

Shiki crouched down and touched the stain with a finger. His finger was red. It was a fresh bloodstain.

6

We will jump a little back in time. The screening at Moro's home theatre which started at seven-thirty proceeded as planned. The clock turned to eight o'clock, then nine o'clock and the film was about to enter its climactic ending.

There are probably very few people who know about the major minor film that is *Massacre Manor*. A more detailed explanation of the film might have been desirable at this point, but the story of this epic film could easily fill a whole tome, making it difficult to provide a concise summary. Instead of a summary, let's take a look at Ryūhei's own impression of the film.

Massacre Manor is basically a film where a lot of people die. A diverse group of people happens to meet at a manor, where they are killed one by one. It may not be realistic, but it's common enough in detective fiction.

Very few people could avoid noticing that the film was taking its cues from Agatha Christie's *And Then There Were None*.

Earlier it was mentioned that the films that created the mystery film boom of the seventies were mainly adaptations of Seishi Yokomizo's and Seichō Matsumoto's work, but there was one more name that shouldn't be overlooked: Agatha Christie.

Films like *Murder on the Orient Express*, *Death on the Nile,* and *The Mirror Crack'd* featured (formerly) great stars like Ingrid Bergman, Elizabeth Taylor and Lauren Bacall. Some called these films "tomb digging films" because of the unique casting.

Massacre Manor also featured a cast of former star actors. It was obvious it had been made to cash in on the mystery boom.

Seven murders were committed in total. The killer was quite busy.

Who is the murderer? What is their motive? It was hard to make a suspenseful film revolving around these questions with just one or two murders, which is probably why they went for seven.

No wonder the film has a runtime of two and a half hours, Ryūhei thought as he watched.

And, as was to be expected from this type of film, the shocking ending revealed that the person thought to be the sixth victim was actually the murderer. Well, to people who know their mystery films, that was hardly shocking.

Ryūhei felt secretly relieved that at least the detective didn't turn out to be the murderer. That was a pattern you also saw too often.

Looking at the film overall, it's definitely fair to say it was stuffed too full, as both a film as well as a mystery story. But you'd be wrong if you assumed Ryūhei thought the film boring. The opposite in fact. Ryūhei liked the film.

All the murder scenes had been designed elaborately and with a lot of variation: there had been a stabbing, a strangling, a poisoning, a fall, etc. You could say the film was like a box of assorted biscuits, offering a bit of every kind.

Ryūhei also liked how the segments between the murders, focusing on human drama, had been kept very brief.

It was not a deep film, but that gave the story a good pace, offering the viewer no time to get bored.

Ryūhei had always questioned the necessity of human drama story elements in mystery films about serial murders.

Complex interpersonal relations may be important to a good mystery story, but it was not unusual for a story to have just too much exposition of the characters' interconnections, resulting in a mystery tale that simply didn't work out.

Ryūhei was of the opinion that *Massacre Manor* had at least managed to avoid this trap.

It was a film that did what the title suggested: betting everything on presenting the viewer with captivating murders. These were Ryūhei's impressions of the film.

Of course, every viewer has their own opinions of a film. Ryūhei had noticed that Moro, who sat next to him, had yawned loudly a few times during the screening. The flick probably didn't appeal to him.

And so the film ended without any interruptions.

Ryūhei stretched his back on the couch.

'That was a lot of fu—,' Ryūhei started, but he was interrupted by Moro.

'It's still only ten o'clock. How about a drink?'

'Yes, great, let's have a few!'

Ryūhei had been invited to Moro's theatre several times now, but not once had he left without having some drinks first. Naturally, Ryūhei had expected that they'd have something to drink after watching this evening's film too.

'All right, I'll buy us some drinks and snacks.'

'No, I'll go! There's a convenience store nearby, isn't there?' Ryūhei offered to his host.

'The convenience stores around here don't carry liquor. But there's a liquor store I always visit. I'll go, you can stay here and read some magazines.'

'Oh, thank you.'

In the corner of the home theatre stood a bookcase filled with magazines. Magazines about films, of course. *KinemaJunpo*, *Scenario*, *Image Forum* and more: the bibles for any film buff in Japan. You could spend a whole day just paging through this collection.

'Oh, and…'

'Yes?'

'Don't touch the equipment.'

It was Moro's usual warning. Moro really didn't let anybody touch any of the equipment in his home theatre. That is why he always warns his guests whenever he has to leave the room.

'Okay, don't worry.'

'I'll be right back.'

Moro seemed relieved at Ryūhei's response, and he left the home theatre.

But. although Moro said he'd be right back, he didn't return right away. He was going to the liquor store, but how far could that be? Surely not in a different part of the city?

Ryūhei was getting worried when the massive door of the home theatre opened. It was Moro. He was holding a plastic bag with the words "Hanaoka Liquors" printed on it. The slender neck of a sake bottle was visible through the opening of the bag.

'Sorry it took so long,' Moro said as he looked at the video player. 'Has it been fifteen minutes? I'm really sorry, something happened.'

The digital clock of the video player was indicating ten-fifteen.

He bowed a few times by way of an apology, and switched on the CD player at the end of the row of audio equipment. Hard rock music blasted out of the speakers.

Ryūhei didn't know much about music, but he knew Moro mostly listened to Aerosmith and Ayako Fuji, and this was probably Aerosmith. He was right, of course.

The silent home theatre immediately became a lot livelier. It was a bit noisy even. It was late already, so Ryūhei was worried whether the neighbours would come complaining.

'Perhaps you shouldn't play hard rock music so loud at this time…'

'Don't worry, this room is completely sound-proof. It's not just for watching films, you know. It's a room for films, rock music, and late night parties.'

'Aha!'

Whenever Ryūhei had small drinking parties with his friends at his own shabby flat, the neighbours would always complain. But that was of course not the case in this particular room.

'I didn't get anything special, but have whatever you want,' said Moro as he took out the liquor and the snacks from the bag. Two bottles of the refined sake Kiyomori. Two cans of *chūhai* (sake mixed with fruit-flavoured carbonated water). Peanuts and small crescent-shaped fried rice crackers. Potato crisps. Salami slices. Cheese *tara* (cheese & cod sticks). Pistachios. More than enough for the two of them.

'Let's have a toast with the *chūhai* first. Say something.'

'Me? Err, well, it's nothing special, but to our health and future. Is that okay?'

'Sure, sure. Okay, to our health and future!'

'Cheers!'

Ryūhei raised his can of *chūhai* high as he yelled energetically. His future may still be uncertain, but at the very least, he had few worries about his health for the time being.

Ryūhei then decided to ask Moro the question that had been lingering on his mind for a few minutes now. 'What did you mean by "something happened"? You mentioned that when you came back.'

'Oh, that? There was some incident.'

Moro took a few sips from his *chūhai* before he continued. 'Hanaoka Liquors is close by, and right across the street there's this place called Takano Apartments.'

'Huh, Taka… huh!?' Ryūhei couldn't believe his ears.

'Takano Apartments.'

'Err, yes, sure.'

Ryūhei could feel his heart beating faster. Ryūhei knew Takano Apartments better than his own neighbourhood bakery. Yuki Konno, the woman who had dumped him in that awful manner, lived there.

Nearly a whole month had passed since they had separated. She was of course not the kind of sensitive girl who would move simply because she broke up with someone, so she was still living there. Ryūhei had not set foot there since their fight.

'What about that place?' Ryūhei kept his shock hidden and urged Moro to continue.

'So when I went to Hanaoka's, there was a crowd right in front of Takano Apartments.'

'Oh.'

'And there were police cars there too.'

'Police cars? Did they catch a burglar?'

'No, apparently someone jumped off the building to commit suicide.'

'What!? Don't tell me it's…' Ryūhei started, but then went silent. He almost said Yuki Konno's name, but what use would it be asking this question of Moro? They didn't know each other.

'What's the matter?' Moro looked puzzled at Ryūhei's reaction.

'Oh, err, nothing hahaha, a suicide isn't really rare nowadays, eh, hahaha.'

His laugh echoed awkwardly in the room. Ryūhei realised it was pretty hard to laugh without a good reason. All kinds of thoughts were racing through his mind. Could Yuki have committed suicide? No, it had to be someone else. But he couldn't help but feel anxious. Yet it couldn't be Yuki, could it?

Moro couldn't know about the internal discussion Ryūhei was having with himself, so he continued: 'No, suicides don't happen often around here, actually. Let alone a suicide by jumping off a building. Mr. Hanaoka himself seemed quite surprised too. So I sort of stuck around to have a look.'

'Rubbernecking?'

'Well, perhaps I did. You know how it is, you see a crowd, so you go and see what's going on. Like when you see a waiting line in front of a shop and feel like joining it.'

'Hahaha, it's not as if you were near a noodle restaurant, hahaha! And what did you see?'

Ryūhei couldn't let it go. Who was it that died? He needed to learn that first.

'Oh, I didn't catch a thing. It's not as if they let the victim lie there for everyone to see. Anyway, that's why it took me a quarter of an hour just to buy some snacks and drinks. Not really much of a serious reason, though. What's the matter, you look pale?'

'It's nothing, I...' Ryūhei suddenly thought of something. 'I think I'm going out for a second. I want to take a look there too.'

'What, really?' A grimace appeared on Moro's face. 'Don't man, that's just being an awful disaster tourist. Well, I guess I was one, too. But I'm serious. You shouldn't go out just to have a look. All you'll see are the backs of other people's heads and the cops trying to keep everyone away.'

'But I want to know who died,' Ryūhei finally confessed.

'Probably just a lonely old person, or an office worker who got fired. You know those stories from the news.'

Moro seemed to have enough of this story and drank the remainder of his *chūhai* in one gulp.

'I guess you're right.'

Chances were that Moro's guess was right. No, it had to be. Tomorrow's paper would have a small article in the corner about an office worker who committed suicide after being sacked. Happens all the time. Nothing special about that at all. Ryūhei was trying to convince himself. Suddenly he thought to himself, why was he feeling so anxious?

His ex-girlfriend lived in Takano Apartments, and there was a suicide there. That was all there was to it. There was nothing to indicate that it had been she who had committed suicide. It was probably someone else who had leapt off the building. Why would it be anything else?

If, and only as a hypothetical case, it was truly Yuki Konno who had committed suicide, what about it? Why would he, her ex-boyfriend, feel sad about it?

Anyway, it wasn't true. She wasn't the type of woman who would commit suicide.

If anyone had a reason to commit suicide, it wouldn't be her, the dumper, but him, the dumpee. And he wasn't so fragile as to commit suicide because of that. At worst, he'd drown himself in drinks, hug a sign at the bus stop and keep bothering the taxi driver.... Wait a second... he was pretty fragile.

Ryūhei felt more miserable the longer his mind wandered off.

Anyway, he had reached his conclusion. He wouldn't learn anything by thinking more about this. Ryūhei decided he shouldn't torment himself with such senseless thoughts anymore.

'What's the matter, you haven't taken a single sip. Go on, have a drink.'

And urged on by Moro, Ryūhei returned to his drinking.

They kept chatting for a while. His can of *chūhai* was empty before he knew it.

'Let's start on the sake then. Ah, oh no,' Moro clicked his tongue as he placed his hand on the back of his head.

'Something wrong?'

'Oh, I haven't taken my bath yet.'

As Moro had noted, Ryūhei had been offered a bath the moment he arrived, but Moro himself hadn't had the time yet.

'I was thinking of washing my hair today. But I really shouldn't take a bath while drunk. Makes me sleepy.'

'In the bathtub?'

'Almost drowned once, you know. Really. They said my nose was barely above the water. Had too much to drink then too.'

What a horrible story. Though Ryūhei couldn't believe you could really drown like that.

'You don't have to mind me, go take your bath. I unplugged the tub when I got out, so all you need to do is fill it again.'

'Ah, okay then. What time is it now?'

'Ten-thirty,' replied Ryūhei after checking the digital clock on the video player.

'Ten-thirty? I still have to fill the tub and, if I want to take my time and relax, then it'll be after eleven by the time I'm done. Perhaps I should just take a shower then, I can't have you waiting for me all the time.'

'No, no, I really don't mind at all.'

'Okay, you can just take whatever you want from the table. I'll try to keep it short. Sorry.'

Moro bowed his head a few times to Ryūhei as he left the home theatre again.

'Take your time!' Ryūhei cried out from behind Moro. There was nothing out of the ordinary about Moro's retreating figure. They'd be wasting time talking about stupid things again in another ten, fifteen minutes. Those were the events of the near future as Ryūhei imagined them to be at that moment.

7

However, Moro did not return in ten minutes, nor even fifteen.

Meanwhile, Ryūhei was feeling quite relaxed all alone in the home theatre and his mind was completely focused on reading the magazines. The series of columns in *KinemaJunpo* by a certain famous film critic about the state of Japanese cinema was very interesting indeed. Ryūhei had started reading from the latest issue, but after getting hooked, he had worked his way back in time, from the February (1st half) issue to the January (2nd half) issue, January (1st half) issue, etc. He had completely forgotten about the time. No, that wasn't the only thing he had forgotten.

When he finally snapped back, he realised that half of the Kiyomori bottle was already gone. Not only that, he had started on quite a lot of the various snacks too. He had felt so at home here, he had taken a lot more than he had first intended. Moro may have said he could take whatever he wanted, but at this rate, he'd think Ryūhei was the sort of guy to actually take advantage of that.

'Oh man, I shouldn't have,' Ryūhei first thought, but then he realised something else wasn't quite right, either.

How long was Moro going to stay in the shower? Wasn't it about time for him to return? Who would go and take a long shower knowing they have a guest waiting in the other room? Ryūhei always thought Moro was a guy with good manners.

Ryūhei finally checked the clock. It was already eleven o'clock. That meant Moro had been in the shower for thirty minutes already. Would anyone take such a long shower?

But then Ryūhei became afraid Moro had had some kind of accident.

That was quite possible. For example, he could have had a dizzy spell in the bathroom and slipped. Or he could have decided to take a bath anyway, and perhaps he had fallen asleep whilst lying comfortably in water up to his shoulders. Wait, the bathtub itself may not be a problem, but it was incredibly dangerous to fall asleep while lying in water! He may only have had one can of *chūhai*, but the liquor was already in his body by the time he headed for the bathroom. Ryūhei just knew something bad had happened.

Worried, Ryūhei got up. The fact that he staggered for a moment showed that he was already intoxicated himself. He did like his drink, but he couldn't drink much. With unsteady steps, Ryūhei made his way to the heavy door and opened it to get into the hallway.

Out of the sound-proof room, Ryūhei could suddenly hear the sound of running water. He knew instantly it was the noise of water from the shower hitting the tiles in the bathroom. Did that mean Moro was having his shower safely?

Besides a running shower, Ryūhei could also hear the noise of a revving motorcycle outside. Was someone doing maintenance on their bike at this hour? For a second, Ryūhei thought about what a nuisance it must be for the neighbours, but then he remembered he had other business to attend to.

'Hello?'

Ryūhei stuck his head inside the dressing room as he called out to Moro. There was a washing machine placed there, as well as a small sink. The remaining floor was lined with planks. Ryūhei stepped inside.

The bathroom was on the other side of the double sliding glass doors. Ryūhei called Moro's name once again.

But once again, there was no response. There was only the monotonous sound of running water. Perhaps Moro hadn't heard Ryūhei because of the water? A third, louder attempt followed.

'Hello? Can you hear me?'

Pang! An explosive exhaust noise came from the motorcycle outside. Be quiet, think of the time, Ryūhei snapped in his mind. But there was still no reply from the bathroom. Something had to be wrong. Had he fallen asleep in the tub? Or had he been overcome by a dizzy spell? Anyway, it was an emergency situation. Ryūhei placed his hand on the knob of the glass sliding door. He found the door was unlocked and slid open smoothly.

Ryūhei could hardly see inside the bathroom, as the whole room was filled with steam. But it did not take long for him to notice the anomaly. It was a scene he had not expected at all.

Moro was lying coiled up on the tiled floor of the bathroom, head down. Hot water was running from the shower head hanging on the hook on the wall. The water was hitting Moro's body and the tiles around him relentlessly, splashing all over the room.

But what shocked Ryūhei the most was that Moro wasn't naked, but still dressed in his clothes. His grey fleece jacket was soaked in water and appeared almost black.

Moro was lying on the bathroom floor looking just as he had when he had left the theatre room earlier. So, had he had a dizzy spell whilst in the shower? Wait... had he really just fainted?

Because if he had only passed out, shouldn't the warm water hitting his face all this time have woken him up by now? So the fact he didn't react at all was... For a moment, Ryūhei was utterly flabbergasted. What had happened in this room?

'Hey, are you okay?'

Ryūhei quickly turned the shower off and tried to raise Moro's body. At that moment, he was hit by a bone-chilling revelation.

It was not at all what he had expected. Moro's body was completely limp. His face lacked any expression. His body felt warm, but was it truly his own body temperature, or had the body just been kept warm by the running shower?

Ryūhei tried looking for a pulse by touching Moro's exposed neck. But he couldn't find any. No. It couldn't be. Ryūhei started to panic. This couldn't be happening.

'He-he's dead! How!?'

Ryūhei howled as his eyes darted around the room. His eyes fell on the drain hole in the corner of the floor. The water that had been washing Moro's body until moments ago was forming one single stream towards the drain hole.

Ryūhei felt his heart jump. There was a hint of red in the stream of water. What's that red? Could it be... could it be blood?

Ryūhei started to search Moro, who was of course still dressed. Moro had been lying face-down, so Ryūhei turned him over. After the face, he started checking the neck, the chest and the stomach, in that order.

The stomach and right side area of Moro's fleece jacket had clearly been stained dark. The grey looked more like a dark red, no, almost black even.

Fearfully Ryūhei took a closer look and even touched the spot with his hand. His finger was immediately stained red.

Ryūhei felt sick. He mustered up all his courage to move Moro's body a bit, so he could have a better look at Moro's right side. There was clearly a tear in the jacket there.

At that moment, there was the ominous sound of something hard touching the tiled floor.

Ryūhei turned his head to get a look inside the tear in the jacket. There was a knife there! He hadn't seen it earlier because Moro's body had been lying on top of it.

The blade was thin and twelve or thirteen centimetres long. But it looked quite sharp.

It was more than obvious now what had happened.

Moro had died because he had been stabbed in his right side through his fleece jacket with this knife. He had been killed! This was a murder! There was no other explanation possible!

By this time Ryūhei was in an absolute panic. Logical thinking and taking action after calm deliberation were impossible for him now. He could only feel an indescribable sensation taking over.

Ryūhei got away from the body and staggered out of the bathroom. And then...

Ryūhei himself couldn't recall exactly what happened then. Apparently, he passed out in the dressing room. He didn't even know whether he just felt dizzy or whether he tripped.

In a film, the screen would now suddenly shake and become unfocused, and fade out. A technique often used in older films. You don't really see it used all that much nowadays.

Anyway, the unconscious Ryūhei obviously did not flee the scene nor did he alert the police. All he did was waste time.

CHAPTER THREE: THE SECOND DAY

1

Man, that was a nasty dream. He hadn't seen dead people appear in his dreams since that one time he thought he'd have fun with Masahiko Ueno's *Corpses are Alive*, a non-fiction book by a medical examiner about bodies and the secrets they hold about the crimes that got them killed. This was the second time. But why did he have a dream like that again?

Oh, that was it, he was watching that film last night, *Massacre Something*. About people getting killed one after another. That was the reason. Probably. But the dream he had last night was far more realistic than the one he'd had before. He could vividly recall the incredibly convincing sensation of touching the body. It didn't feel like a dream, more like very detailed footage.

A dead body in the bathroom. Blood flowing into the drain hole. A knife lying on the floor. It was a dream straight out of Hitchcock. In *Psycho*, it was more a shower room than a bathroom though. And the victim there was an attractive woman, Janet Leigh her name was. But there were no attractive women in his dream.

Eh? Who was the body in his dream again? It was someone he knew. Ah, it was Kōsaku Moro. Yep, it that's who it was. Why did he die? Moro was the last guy he wanted to see dead.

'Ah!'

It wasn't a dream. The random images in his mind eventually brought him back to the cold reality. Ryūhei finally realised he was lying on the planks of the dressing room. They gave off a chemical smell. He opened his eyes to a surprise. It was a sight few persons are ever likely to see: the legs of a washing machine.

It didn't take long for Ryūhei to realise what he was doing and where. He was lying on the floor next to the washing machine in the dressing room in Moro's place.

He raised his head first, followed by the rest of his body. He felt so stiff all over he was surprised he didn't creak. His neck in particular hurt. Must have been his sleeping posture.

'Uuugh, it hurts.'

He put his hand to his neck and grimaced.

It was dark. Was it still night? No, it had to be morning. He could faintly make out some light. But something was not right.

It was then that Ryūhei noticed what was wrong. The lights in the room were not on. Last night, he had fainted after discovering the body. So, obviously, he had not switched off the light. And yet the lights in the dressing room were off. And not just here. It was dark in the bathroom, in the hallway, everywhere. Had someone else switched the lights off?

Ryūhei tried the switch, but nothing happened.

'Blackout?'

Ryūhei then remembered that the weather forecast last night said there might be thunderstorms. The lightning must have caused a power outage whilst he was unconscious.

Anyway, Ryūhei wanted to know what time it was. He raised his left arm to look at his wristwatch, but there was only the sleeve of his sweatshirt. He recalled he had taken his watch off when he took his bath last night, and had put it in the pocket of his jeans.

Ryūhei got up from the floor unsteadily and started searching the pockets of his jeans, which had been dumped in a basket on top of the washing machine. The cheap watch he pulled out was indicating nine-thirty. He counted back and realised he must have been lying on the floor for about ten hours. It had been a complete waste of time, but what could he do about that now?

Was his head throbbing because of the booze last night? Or because he had hit his head on the floor when he fell?

Whatever the cause, his head hurt. If possible, he would like to lie down for a little longer. Preferably in a soft large bed this time, where he could stretch out. But that was a wish that couldn't come true for the moment.

If the nightmarish sight he saw last night had not been a nightmare, he had no time to lose. But at that moment, Ryūhei hesitated. Had that really been reality? Somewhere inside, Ryūhei still couldn't believe it. Had Moro really died?

'Let it be a dream! I call upon you, the gods and the buddhas and eternal dragons and the whole gang!'

Eternal dragons probably weren't going to do much for him, but Ryūhei felt he had to plead to some deity before he'd go in. He needed to talk some courage into himself first. Slowly he peered through the half-open doors into the bathroom. Let it be a normal, peaceful, empty bathroom! Grant my wish!

Unfortunately, what awaited him was the same sight as last night.

It was the exact same scene, save for the fact the steam was gone and the body seemed a few hours older. Moro had been stabbed to death last night and had been lying here since. Poor fellow. But it had only turned out like this because Ryūhei had passed out. So he shouldn't be wasting even more time now.

'I'll have to call the police first.'

Ryūhei exited the bathroom and made his way to the living room via the hallway. The telephone was in the living room. He had just extended his right hand to lift up the receiver when he thought of something. He retracted his hand. Fingerprints. What if the murderer's fingerprints were on the receiver? If he carelessly picked it up, he might mess things up greatly for when the investigators came later.

Furthermore, Ryūhei had never called the emergency number 110 even once in his life. That's only normal, of course. But Ryūhei never liked talking on the phone. To be honest, he just didn't have enough courage to dial 110.

He thought about running to the nearest police box. It was only a minute from the White Wave Apartments to the nearest one. It would be faster than having him stammer on the phone. And, to be honest, he couldn't bear staying any longer in this flat. Those were his true feelings.

Ryūhei changed his clothes in a hurry. He put his wristwatch on, hurled the sweatshirt and sweatpants into the washing machine, and proceeded to the entrance hall.

The black coat which had lost its master was still hanging from the hook on the wall there. Ryūhei quickly put his shoes on in front of the nondescript but sturdy iron door, with its metal door knob. He took out a handkerchief and used it to cover the door knob as he turned it, so as to preserve any fingerprints that might be on it. Ryūhei took the matter very seriously.

He turned the knob and pushed the heavy door open. The door creaked as it moved. But the next moment, Ryūhei was confronted with an unbelievable sight.

A chain was stretched straight only a few dozen centimetres in front of Ryūhei's eyes. It was the door chain. The door couldn't be opened any farther. The front door had been completely locked from the inside. But who had done that? That was a complete mystery.

How should one describe Ryūhei's surprise? It's like the feeling when you were sure you could just make it beneath the lowering bar of the railway crossing, but then it turned out you couldn't. Or when you didn't doubt for a second you could just pass the automatic turnstile, but then got hit hard in the knees. No, no, that's still minor compared to what Ryūhei was experiencing. Why was this door locked from the inside!? The fact there was nobody around to give the answer to Ryūhei's question only strengthened his confusion.

The two words "locked room" suddenly popped up in his mind. But it was still too soon to be sure about that. He first had to check whether there weren't other ways to exit the flat besides through the front door.

Ryūhei put his plans to go to the police on hold for the moment, and shut the door.

He traced his steps back to the living room, where he took a good look at his surroundings. The only other exit out of the living room was the one sash window leading to the veranda. Moro's place was on the ground floor, so you were all clear once you were out on the veranda. But why did the murderer who stabbed Moro not leave the flat through the front door, choosing instead the unusual escape route via the veranda? Ryūhei ignored this fundamental problem for the moment, and examined the window.

It took him less than five seconds.

The window had a common crescent sash lock. A single look was enough to confirm it had been completely and perfectly locked. There was also no unusual gap between the window and the frame. So even if the killer had escaped through this window, they could not have locked the crescent lock from the outside. It was therefore not feasible that the murderer had used it as an escape route. Another window then?

Ryūhei returned to the bathroom. He remembered there was a window there too. But the tilting window was obviously only there for daylight and air circulation. Even when opened completely, the gap created only measured about ten centimetres. It was obvious that it would be utterly impossible for any human being to escape through it. Ryūhei silently pulled the half-open window shut again. He was worried someone outside might see him.

Ryūhei then moved to the home theatre, but there were no windows there whatsoever. The room originally had a sash window, just as in the living room, but that window was now hidden behind the projection screen. And the window was not just covered by the screen. Moro had sound-proofed the room by covering all the walls with some excellent isolation material, so the window had been completely sealed off. It probably violated some disaster regulations, but it was a perfect anti-burglar measure. Escaping from the room through the window was also out of the question.

Ryūhei didn't have high expectations as he went into the kitchen. There was a small window there, but that too was locked with a crescent latch. The window was also covered by aluminium grating outside, so even if it had not been locked from the inside, nobody could have got out through it anyway.

The toilet then? Ryūhei opened the door of the toilet, but had to close it again. Like the home theatre, there was no window there in the first place.

The entrance hall, living room, home theatre, bathroom, kitchen, toilet. All the rooms had been checked. No, wait!

Ryūhei suddenly thought of one possibility, a possibility which put him on guard for a second. If this space, consisting of two rooms, a kitchen, bathroom and toilet was completely locked from the inside, and Moro had been stabbed to death in the bathroom, didn't that mean the murderer was still inside?

Logic dictated such a conclusion.

But despite what logic may say, Ryūhei quickly realised it was certainly not a realistic notion, and soon discarded his fears. Moro was killed last night. And it was almost ten in the morning now. Could you ever imagine a murderer hanging around the crime scene for half a day? Unless we were talking about a very patient murderer, it was just not possible.

And, as Ryūhei had been checking all the windows, going through every room, he had found nobody. And there were basically no spots here where one could hide. At best behind the sofa or inside a closet, or… No, that was about it. Just two places. Not a very good home to play hide-and-seek.

Just to be sure, Ryūhei decided to check those two places. But he didn't even come across a cockroach, let alone a killer.

Now, this posed a problem which required a bit of contemplation. Ryūhei got a hold of himself, and decided to sit down on the sofa in the living room to give the conundrum its deserved attention.

It appeared he had found himself inside what is commonly called a locked room. It was probably safe to proclaim that now. Of course, there was nobody there to hear him proclaim anything. Ryūhei could only brood and reflect on the matter all by himself. His internal questioning continued for a while.

The immediate problem occupying his mind was whether he should contact the police or not.

Normally, one should call the police immediately, of course. Even Ryūhei knew that was the duty of any law-abiding citizen. He might not be an exemplary citizen, not by a long shot, but duty is duty.

But hadn't far too much time passed by now for him to play the role of the law-abiding citizen? That was the thing he was worried about. Half a day had already passed since the murder had occurred. What would the police think if Ryūhei were to call them right now?

There was no doubt that the police would view Ryūhei as a suspicious figure. And this was a locked room murder. The only persons inside the flat were Ryūhei and Moro. Given that one of them was the victim, it was only natural that people would assume the other was the killer. Things could become very uncomfortable for Ryūhei. Should he then still perform the duty of a law-abiding citizen, just like that?

Ryūhei could not find the right answer to the question.

So, should he then just unlock the door chain and flee the scene? The locked room would cease to be locked from that point on and, as a result, the police would not be able to automatically build a case to finger Ryūhei as the murderer. Ryūhei didn't have a motive to kill Moro in the first place, so the police might not even view him as a suspect in the case.

Once the police found Moro's body, they would almost certainly contact all the people he knew. They might use some rough-handed methods to get a confession, or perhaps appeal to the murderer's emotional side, but they would probably catch him. And Ryūhei would never have to get involved with any of it.

That would obviously be the perfect scenario for Ryūhei. But would things really go so smoothly?

Probably not. Ryūhei became desperate.

By now Ryūhei's traces were all over the place, and it would be impossible to get rid of all of them. It wasn't just his fingerprints. His hair was probably in the bathroom as well. The police's forte is forensic investigation, so sooner or later, they'd become aware of Ryūhei's existence. It was unlikely they would shrug and walk away if he said he was sorry and that he just hadn't wanted to get involved. One way or another, they'd come to view him as a suspect.

So what should he do?

Seeing no way out, Ryūhei decided to seek advice from a friend. Perhaps because some wise words that had been the slogan of a radio life counselling program suddenly appeared in his head. "Shared joy is a double joy; shared sorrow is half a sorrow."

2

Ryūhei took his notebook from his day bag and stared at it. He chose Yūji Makita's number from the short list of his friends, because they were close, and Makita was quite good at swiftly handling matters.

Ryūhei hesitantly dialled the number. The phone rang a few times. They never answer your call right away when it's an emergency. Just when Ryūhei thought he would have to let that damn phone ring until eternity, his call was answered.

'Yes?'

Yūji Makita always betrayed himself with his unique voice. Ryūhei felt a moment of relief. He felt cheered on by the voice of his friend.

'Makita? It's me, Tomura.'

'Ryūhei? What's the matter, you sound like you're in a hurry.'

Ryūhei thought he had been talking normally, but apparently, he couldn't hide how distressed he truly was.

'Ah, well, you see, err, how should I put it...' Ryūhei stammered. How should he explain what was going on? 'I think I'm in trouble. Like, big trouble.'

'Ah, I thought so.'

Ryūhei also cried out at Makita's nonchalant reply. The receiver almost fell from his hand and he barely managed to hold on. He tried to feign calmness again.

'You thought so? What do you mean, what do you know?'

'I heard about it just now,' Makita said in a monotonous voice. 'Awful thing happened.'

'O—oh.' Ryūhei couldn't understand a word of what Makita said. 'Err, did someone tell you about it?'

'Yes, two police detectives were here just now.'

'The police?'

'Huh, they haven't paid you a visit yet?'

Ryūhei's brain was working at full speed to process the meaning of Makita's answers. "Something awful" "Two police detectives" and "They haven't paid you a visit yet?" Apparently, something big had happened that was connected to Ryūhei. But it couldn't be connected to the fact Moro was lying coldly on the bathroom floor. There was no way that the authorities were already busy with the investigation into Moro's murderer. The body was still here, lying on the tiles in the bathroom next door. But only Ryūhei knew that.

So what were those two detectives investigating? Why had they talked with Yūji Makita?

While still confused by the sudden turn of events, Ryūhei tried to answer Makita's questions.

'They haven't come to me yet. They'll probably be here soon.'

'Of course they'll see you, she was your girlfriend.'

Ryūhei's heart almost jumped out of his chest.

'My girlfriend….!'

'Oh, sorry, sorry,' Makita apologised. 'Ex-girlfriend, I should say.'

Yuki Konno! Makita's "awful thing" had not been about Moro, but about Yuki! Even the slow-witted Ryūhei finally managed to connect all the dots now.

Last night, Moro had told him about hearing about someone falling to their death from Takano Apartments whilst he was out buying their drinks. Yuki Konno lived there. And today, the police were talking to the people who knew her. There was only one conclusion possible.

The woman who had fallen to her death from Takano Apartments last night was none other than Yuki Konno.

That would explain why the police were visiting the people who knew her. It was only natural they'd visit Yūji Makita, and of course Yuki's ex-boyfriend, Ryūhei.

'But man, you're in for some trouble, I'm afraid. The police seemed to be suspicious of you. Well, perhaps it's not that odd that they'd suspect the ex-boyfriend, given she fell to her death soon after she broke up with you.'

'Wa—wait a sec! They suspect me? Was she... was Yuki murdered? Wasn't it a suicide?'

'Huh, haven't you read the newspapers?'

'Err, no.'

'She was killed. She was stabbed in the back and then thrown off the balcony of her room. Absolutely horrible. The murderer must have hated her guts.'

'…'

'But it wasn't you, was it? Even though you were really upset that she dumped you.'

'…'

'I—it wasn't you, was it?'

'N—no, of course not!'

The situation was alarming. The utter shock wiped Ryūhei's mind completely blank. He had called Yūji Makita to get advice because Moro was murdered, but now he learned he had become a suspect in the case of the death of Yuki Konno. Shared sorrow is half a sorrow? His sorrow had doubled!

Feeling horribly miserable, Ryūhei didn't even feel like talking anymore.

'Hey, Ryūhei, what's the matter? You okay?'

'Oh, err, yes, thank you. I'll talk to you later.'

'Hey.'

'Huh?'

'Didn't you call me to ask me something?'

'Oh, no, it's nothing. I just wanted to talk with someone about Yuki's death. Later.'

Ryūhei made up an excuse and quickly replaced the receiver before Makita could say anything. In the end, Ryūhei hadn't even mentioned Moro. Man, why had he made that call in the first place?

He had learnt the news that Yuki Konno had fallen to her death, but his own situation had not improved one bit. It had even worsened .

At this very moment, he was already suspected of being connected to Yuki's death. And once they discovered Moro's body in the bathroom, it was only natural they'd suspect him of that murder as well. Double trouble. Even the carefree Ryūhei saw little hope in the near future. At this rate, he'd be arrested. And there were no guarantees that his innocence could be proved.

He was overcome with a sense of terror he had never experienced.

The action Ryūhei then decided to take would only further confuse the rest of the story. Ryūhei would later come to regret his foolish action, but at that point in time, he had not considered the consequences.

Ryūhei quickly wiped his fingerprints off the receiver. He started wiping all the places he remembered he had touched between last night and this morning with his handkerchief: the couch, the table, the door knob, the windows, the light switches, etc. He didn't wipe everything 100% of course, because there was no need. Ryūhei often visited Moro, so a few of his fingerprints here and there wouldn't pose any problems. But there couldn't be too many of them. The police could probably easily guess when his last visit had taken place, based on the number of fingerprints.

He went into the home theatre, and wiped everything there as well. The videotape of *Massacre Manor* lying on top of the video player was also placed in his day bag.

Once he had finished there, he put all the remaining sake, the empty cans of *chūhai* and the half-eaten snacks in the plastic bag from

Hanaoka Liquors. It was a waste, but the unopened bottle of sake and snacks also went inside the bag. He carefully tied the bag tight and held it in his right hand.

No explanation is probably necessary at this point. Ryūhei had decided to flee from a flat where a murder had taken place. "Flee" is perhaps even too mild a description. Perhaps it would be more accurate to say he made a run for it.

Running away from the crime scene was of course not only a cowardly thing to do, it would only worsen his own situation. It was the worst thing he could possibly have done.

But people do tend to make the worst possible decisions when in desperate situations.

Ryūhei may have realised that deep down inside, but he lacked the courage to face the truth.

He ran outside holding his day bag and the plastic bag, which he intended to throw away somewhere. His wristwatch showed it was already past ten-thirty.

3

Ryūhei fled the scene at full speed. But the people in town who saw him and knew nothing about what had happened, probably only saw a young man who was speed walking.

Which was understandable. A man sprinting at full speed through town without any clear reason would only attract attention.

The contradictory feelings of wanting to pretend that nothing was wrong and not stand out, and the wish to get away as fast as possible clashed as Ryūhei walked, and occasionally ran, away.

As he crossed Saiwaichō park near the apartment building, he threw the plastic bag away in one of the garbage cans. Similar-looking bags had already been thrown in, so Ryūhei's bag immediately disappeared amongst the other bags. Perfect, he thought.

As he took another look, he noticed, amongst the plastic bottles and plastic bags, a brand-new newspaper which had been folded up neatly. He pulled it out and checked the date. As he had expected: it was today's morning paper.

According to Yūji Makita, the incident at Takano Apartments had been in the paper. And the newspapers had said it had not been an accident, but a murder.

Ryūhei could feel his heart beat loudly as he timidly opened the paper. His eyes swiftly scanned the general news pages from corner to corner, but he couldn't find an article about the deadly fall of a college student.

Then he realised it might be in the local news section. He took a look there, and there it was!

College Student Falls To Mysterious Death

At 09:45 p.m. on the 28th, the body of college student Yuki Konno (20) was discovered in front of Takano Apartments in Saiwaichō. She had fallen to her death from the flat, where she lived on the third floor. She had been discovered by an office worker who happened to pass by and immediately notified the nearby police box. Patrol officers immediately rushed to the scene, but Konno could not be saved.

Police investigation revealed that she sustained not only wounds from her fall, but that she had also been stabbed in the back with a knife-like instrument. The police therefore are treating her death as a homicide.

So it really was a murder.

Ryūhei once again felt a sense of shock. When Moro had told him about the incident last night, it had seemed like an accidental fall, or perhaps a suicide. But the truth was different.

'Nine forty-five last night...'

Ryūhei tried to recall what he was doing at that time. Ah, at nine forty-five last night he was watching *Massacre Manor* with Moro. It took him a while to remember something that simple.

Just as the film was entering its climactic conclusion, Yuki Konno was being murdered at nearby Takano Apartments.

The realisation gave him a weird sensation. Those two events seemed so far apart that they couldn't have occurred on the same night in the same town. It made Ryūhei feel as if he and Yuki had been far apart last night, whilst in reality, Takano Apartments and White Wave Apartments were only a one-minute walk away through Saiwaichō Park.

Even whilst he was reading the news in the paper, Ryūhei thought the whole business felt untrue, devoid of any sense of reality. This was probably not because of the news of Yuki's death, but because he himself had been confronted with the bloody scene of Moro's death.

Ryūhei's current situation could perhaps only be described as stupefying. About ninety minutes after his ex-girlfriend Yuki Konno met her demise last night, Ryūhei himself was confronted with the murder of Kōsaku Moro.

Had anyone ever experienced a worse night?

And the worst part was that, whilst Ryūhei had a perfect alibi for the time of Yuki's murder, he could not present it. For the witness to his alibi, Moro, was not of this world anymore.

Ryūhei had to be the unluckiest man on the planet.

The greatest misfortune to befall him was that the police were now after him. And there was no way for him to ignore this truth. Ryūhei had to admit that even he would suspect himself if he had been a police detective and heard his story. He knew very well how bad his situation looked.

Ryūhei finally decided what to do.

First, he'd run. Nothing good would happen if the police were to catch him. He couldn't think of any way to prove his own innocence. The only option left to him was to flee.

Ryūhei chose to take busy streets with lots of people as much as possible. Yet he couldn't help but fear that any one of the people passing by could be a police officer. Takano Apartments was very close by, so there was a definite danger he'd come across one. Would a uniformed officer appear suddenly to restrain him? Ryūhei's heart was racing as he walked the streets in fear.

After a while, he couldn't bear the anxiety anymore and stepped inside a telephone box. He needed an accomplice in his flight. He decided to ask someone for help.

That someone was a man, age thirty-four. Their relationship? The man was the ex-husband of Ryūhei's older sister, so he was Ryūhei's ex-brother-in-law. So basically, they weren't in any way related now.

But his occupation was private detective.

Some readers might find it odd that Ryūhei would suddenly think of asking a detective for help in his time of crisis. They might be thinking the idea came out of nowhere.

'A private eye? What a joke! Those fictional heroes only exist in mystery novels, or film noir,' they may be saying to themselves.

And that's the common view, perhaps. Even people living in large cities are not likely ever to have seen the sign of a detective agency as they stroll through the streets. They might pass convenience stores, drug stores, fast food chains filled with youngsters or noodle restaurants with lines waiting in front, but detective agencies? No.

No wonder many people assume there are no such things as private detectives or detective agencies in Japan, and that they can only be found in the United States.

I'd like to ask those people to flip through the telephone directory. No, not the blue one for non-commercial numbers. The yellow one. The yellow pages.

Go to the "D" section. There's "dance schools" and "day care centres". And also "dairy products" and "data processing". Perhaps we should move on to "De" entries. "Decorators" "dental clinics" "dermatologists" and there it is, "Detectives". Of course, you could also look for "Investigators" under "I". Both entries should bring up the same pages. So, let's take a look there.

By the way, Ryūhei was at that moment flipping through the Ikagawa City Region telephone directory. It's a thick book of over eight-hundred pages, but the "Investigators/Private Detectives" section alone is surprisingly over ten pages long. That was the proof that, even outside the metropolis of Tōkyō, in a middle-sized city like Ikagawa City, you had literally hundreds of private detectives and investigators.

And there were of course more private detectives than the amount of telephone numbers in the yellow pages. A staggering amount. And that's only in this region, so just imagine how immense the list of numbers must be in areas like Tōkyō and Ōsaka.

Scale may be a different matter, but in terms of numbers, private detectives were definitely not rare in cities. There were probably also many people who made use of them.

But to change the topic for a moment: many people seem to think that private detectives and morticians don't advertise. Ryūhei was one of those people.

Reality however was different. Like other industries, private investigators, too, paid much attention to promoting themselves.

Some large detective agencies have advertisements with a photograph of their headquarters to display their organisational and operational abilities, while also featuring famous actors as brand ambassadors to instil a sense of trustworthiness and confidence. You can imagine how successful those campaigns are and how the phones never stop ringing.

But the private detective Ryūhei was hoping to reach now did not belong to any of those major agencies. He worked alone, and ran his own private detective agency. So, sadly enough, he could only dream of the major advertisement campaigns of the larger agencies. Ryūhei had visited his detective agency a few times, a shabby place located on the second floor of a multi-tenant building. His operational capabilities were nothing worth mentioning. His organisational abilities were zero. He had nothing going for him.

That is why he had decided he should at least have a catchy slogan. "Detectives Don't Sleep" or something like that.

The advertisement the detective had put in the yellow pages was about the size of a large business card and said the following:

Morio Ukai Detective Agency
Welcome Trouble!
TEL: XX-XXX-XXXX

"Welcome trouble" was a line the deceased film critic Nagaharu Yodogawa often used. It was pretty good as a slogan for a detective agency.

The truth is that the person who thought of this slogan was none other than Ryūhei. As you can see, the bond between the Ukai Detective Agency and Ryūhei was as thick as blood. And, as mentioned earlier, Ukai was Ryūhei's dear ex-brother-in-law. He was the one person Ryūhei could rely on in the situation he was in.

Ryūhei placed the open telephone directory next to him as he dialled the number. He was ill at ease as the ringback tone continued. Feelings of both expectation and anxiety were struggling inside him.

Ukai's slogan may be "Welcome trouble" but would he really welcome the kind of trouble Ryūhei had got himself into? That question was the source of his distress.

The phone rang a few times before anyone answered.

'Hello, the Morio Ukai Detective Agency here.'

Ryūhei recognised the slightly nasal voice. It was the detective himself. He felt relieved.

'It's me, Ryūhei. It's been a while.'

'Aaaaaaaaaah, aha, aah!'

The curious answer echoed in Ryūhei's ear. It was almost as if the person on the other end had suddenly hurt his jaw.

'Err, it's me, Ryūhei Tomura. You remember me, don't you?'

'Yes, of course, always thankful for your patronage!'

'Huh.' Ryūhei was flabbergasted. 'Wha—what patronage?'

'I'm terribly sorry!'

Ryūhei was so confused by the unexpected apology that he suddenly couldn't utter a word. Ukai continued.

'I have guests here at the moment and, as I need to talk over our business in more detail... I am terribly sorry, but would you mind if I call you back in fifteen minutes? Eh? You will call again? Aha, thank you, I'll be waiting for your call.'

'Wa—wait!'

'I'll be waiting for your call in fifteen minutes. Yes, thank you, goodbye.'

And the call ended.

What just happened? Puzzled, Ryūhei replaced the receiver. He had to think about it for a while, but then he finally understood. The point Ukai was trying to make was that he had "guests" in the office.

So who were those guests? They were probably police. When Ryūhei called Yūji Makita, he had been told the police had just visited Makita. Ryūhei had probably called Ukai right during the police detectives' visit to his office. Their target was of course Ryūhei. It appeared the police were seriously trying to locate him. Ukai knew nothing about how, or if, Ryūhei was connected to Yuki Konno's death, of course.

That's why Ukai acted quickly, and pretended he was on the phone with someone else in order to fool the police.

And Ukai had repeated during the call that he was waiting for his call back in fifteen minutes. That was probably because Ukai guessed the detectives would be gone by then.

Ryūhei waited inside the telephone box for fifteen minutes to pass.

He was afraid that the moment he stepped out of the telephone box, someone would start telling him he'd been in there too long. Ryūhei flipped mindlessly through the telephone directory to kill time. Luckily, there was no line waiting outside the box. When exactly fifteen minutes had passed, Ryūhei once again dialled the Morio Ukai Detective Agency. He was ready to hang up immediately if anyone other than Ukai answered the phone.

'Hello, the Morio Ukai Detective Agency here.'

'It's me, Tomura.'

'Ah, perfect,' said Ukai, sounding satisfied at the other end of the line. 'You're sharp, kid. I have to admit I was afraid you wouldn't call me back. I must have confused you terribly.'

'Yes, I was a bit surprised. But what was the matter over there? You said you had guests... the police?'

The reply was a whistle. Ukai seemed in high spirits.

65

'Full marks for you today. Great guess. Just before you called, two detectives arrived. They said they were investigating the death of a college student last night, Yuki Konno. They wanted to know your whereabouts. I didn't know where you were of course, and I wouldn't have told them even if I had known.'

'And I happened to call you right at that moment.'

'Exactly. I almost cried your name out in surprise. I was literally quaking in my boots. Anyway, the police seem to think you have something to do with Yuki Konno's fall. I don't believe it, of course, but err, did you do something to deserve those suspicions?'

'No, of course not. I haven't done anything. I was just her ex-boyfriend.'

'Oh. But the police mentioned something.'

'Something? What?'

'That you yelled "I'm going to kill yaaaa" while drunk at a station. That did really happen, didn't it?'

'How did the police…!?'

Who was it who told them that!?

'Remember where it happened? There were probably a hundred witnesses there. The next time, think carefully about where you want to cause a scene.'

'…'

Ryūhei suddenly felt the energy ebbing from his body, but he managed to hold on to the receiver.

'A—anyway, I have nothing to do with Yuki's fall. That was probably suicide... ah, no, the newspaper said it was murder. But it wasn't me.'

'Thought so. But then your course of action is simple. You did nothing wrong, so you don't need to go around running and hiding. Just go to the police. It won't be pleasant perhaps, but it's better than being accused of a serious crime. I'll come with you if you'd prefer that.'

'You see, I can't.'

'Something bothering you?'

'Something has happened. How should I put it... I'm in really big trouble. It's not something I can explain over the phone.'

'Hm. I suppose you're dealing with a lot now. Okay then, will you come here? Or should I go to you?'

While Ryūhei would have preferred being picked up where he was by Ukai, he knew he couldn't impose on him too much. Which is why he decided to put on a brave face.

'I'll come to your place.'

'I'll be waiting then,' Ukai responded lightly at first, but then his tone became more serious. 'The entrance to this building may be watched. Use the back exit, and the emergency stairs. That's probably safe.'

'Err, oh, huh…'

'See you then.'

The call was over. Ryūhei had to make his way to the Morio Ukai Detective Agency via a "probably safe" route. He regretted his brave face.

4

The multi-tenant building which housed the Morio Ukai Detective Agency was located behind the train station. You needed to go through a narrow street in a north-easterly direction and then through several alleyways to reach the building, which stood alongside similar ones, all of which were decorated with gaudy neon signs for bars, clubs and other establishments you might expect. The detective agency was located in the outskirts of what you might call the entertainment district.

Ryūhei couldn't work out whether the location was good or bad for Ukai's business. Large detective agencies that sold themselves on trustworthiness and confidence weren't likely to be found here. But it might well be the perfect place for the Ukai Detective Agency, which welcomed trouble.

Ryūhei took a cab to the rear of the train station and walked through the entertainment district.

A slender man with a bowtie tried to lure him with a "morning service" but he ignored him. Ryūhei didn't know what kind of morning service it was, but it did remind him he hadn't had breakfast yet. But the man was probably not offering him toast and coffee. Better forget him. Perhaps another time.

Ryūhei approached the building from the rear entrance, as advised by Ukai. He first took a good look at the surroundings and, when he was sure there was nobody around, he dashed towards the emergency stairs. It was a spiral staircase unfortunately. He went as quickly as possible up to the second floor, pushed the rusty iron door open and slipped inside. He was out of breath and felt dizzy. It's really in times of emergency that a lack of exercise will come back to bite you.

A cold, dark corridor greeted him. He had heard that half of the rooms in the building were empty. It was supposed to become livelier here at night, but it was silent during the day. Ryūhei stopped in front of a door about halfway along the corridor.

There was a white sign with black lettering nailed to the door.

Morio Ukai Detective Agency.

And below that was written "Welcome Trouble". That was all. Which seemed rather dry.

It seemed obvious that the detective in question was not particularly passionate about conducting his business.

Ryūhei rang the bell. The door opened halfway, revealing Ukai's familiar face.

Morio Ukai was the perfect person to be a private detective. He was of average height, had an average build, and nothing about his face stood out. He was not rich in facial expressions which could betray his feelings, so even with the same face, he could look both gentle or scary just by putting on glasses or adjusting his hair. If you put him in a classroom, you would immediately think he was a teacher. As you might guess from his occupation, he was also an expert in impersonating a police detective. If he wore a plain suit with no accessories, he could walk down the street without anyone ever noticing his presence. But if he were to put on the latest fashion, well, it would make him look like a fairly handsome man.

Ukai always said that the greatest weapon a detective had was the ability not to stand out. Secretly, Ryūhei thought that Ukai couldn't stand out, even if he wanted to.

'You made it here pretty quickly. Nobody saw you?'

'I'm pretty sure we're okay,' said Ryūhei, as he quickly stepped inside the office. The heater was on, too much even. The sense of relief and the warm air in the room drained Ryūhei's body of all its tension and stress, and he slumped down into a nearby chair.

'You look tired. I'll make us some coffee first and then we can talk, no hurry. Those police detectives left just now, so they're not likely to return any time soon. You hungry?'

Ryūhei nodded vigorously.

The coffee was blacker than ink and intensely bitter, whilst the baguette that came with it was like thick paper. It was hardly food, but the ink and thick paper disappeared into Ryūhei's stomach within minutes. At that moment, he would even have enjoyed a menu of muddy water and cardboard if it had been served to him. An empty stomach is the best cook, as they say.

'So maybe you can tell me what's the matter? I gather you've got yourself into quite a bit of trouble.'

'Yes, indeed. Here's what happened.'

Ryūhei told Ukai everything that had occurred the previous evening. He told Ukai honestly every detail that he could remember, even repeating every word that had been said as best as he could recall. He used his hands and body to tell his tale. It was like one of those crime scene re-enactment videos, but all played by one person.

The private detective was sitting in his armchair behind the desk, which was littered with documents and writing utensils. He seemed to be listening seriously to Ryūhei's story. He did not interrupt him or ask questions in between.

Once Ryūhei was done, Ukai summarised the events of the night before.

'So basically, last evening, you arrived at Kōsaku Moro's place at seven o'clock. Flat 4 on the ground floor of White Wave Apartments. You had a bath first, and at seven-thirty you watched a film with Moro in his home theatre. The film was *Massacre Manor* by film director Ryūtarō Kawauchi, and your screening ended at ten o'clock.'

'Yes, that's right.'

'Once the video had ended, Moro went out to the liquor store. On his way, he passed by Takano Apartments where someone had fallen to her death and he returned after fifteen minutes. At ten-fifteen, you and Moro started on the *chūhai* and talked about the incident until about ten-thirty. Moro then went to the bathroom alone, whilst you remained in the home theatre, concentrating on old film magazines and drinks. At eleven o'clock, you got worried and went to the bathroom to check on Moro. He had been stabbed to death there. You fainted because of the sheer shock. These were the events of yesterday night.'

'Yes.'

'So now we move on to today. You woke up at nine-thirty. You first checked whether there really was a body, but when you were about to leave the room to notify the police, you noticed the front door had been locked from the inside with the door chain. You also checked every window in the place where anyone could climb out, but they were all locked from the inside. But there was no third person inside the flat either. It was what they call a locked room. You made a phone

69

call to Yūji Makita in the hopes of getting advice, but instead you learned the shocking news of Yuki Konno's death. Then you wiped off your fingerprints throughout the flat and took all your belongings with you as you fled the scene. You threw the snacks and drinks you had last night away in Saiwaichō Park. And then you called me. And that's why you're here now.'

'Yes, that's more or less how it all happened. Man, it's almost like one of those language exams.'

'Exams?'

'Where you have to summarise a story in one hundred and fifty words or less.'

'You don't seem to be taking this seriously. You don't see the peril you're in? You're acting as if this isn't about you.'

'But it really isn't about me!' said Ryūhei sullenly. 'I haven't done anything, I'm not involved with any of this!'

'The police won't think that. But this case certainly has some interesting features. Yes, very interesting.'

'Because it's a locked room murder?'

'That's certainly one reason, but right now you and I are the only ones who are aware that it is in fact a locked room murder. The police don't know that. It's the circumstances that make this case so interesting. Yes, I'm itching to work on it!'

'Err, have you ever worked on a locked room murder before?'

'…'

'So, no.' Apparently, the detective just liked the idea. 'Are you sure you know what to do?'

'Don't worry. Leave it up to me. This agency may be small, but we welcome trouble and have helped countless numbers of clients.'

'I was the one who came up with that "Welcome Trouble" slogan, you know.'

'Err, really? Oh well,' said Ukai as he scratched his head. 'Anyway, I have a few questions for you first.'

'Go ahead.'

'Do you know of anyone who might hold a grudge against Yuki Konno? Besides you, of course.'

That last part irritated Ryūhei.

'I didn't hold any grudge against her.'

'But what about that scene at the station? You were hugging a sign at the bus stop and screaming "Yukiiiii, you damn hussy, I'm going to kill yaaaa!" Or so I've been told.'

'Uuurgh, don't bring that up any more.' Ryūhei quickly interrupted Ukai. 'And I didn't call her a damn hussy. At least, probably not.'

'Are you sure?'

'…'

'See?'

'Daaaamn...'

'I knew it. You said "Damn" again. You were thinking "damn detective!" right? You're surprisingly short-tempered.'

'You were feeding me leading questions! You can't lure people out and then call them short-tempered.'

'Will you admit you held a grudge against Yuki?'

'…Okay, I'll admit it. But I didn't kill her.'

'I know. But is there anyone else who hated her?'

'I don't know. It might just be my imagination, but I think that after she dumped me, she moved on to someone else. Something could have happened between her and her new boyfriend. That would be a motive.'

'That's only if that person actually exists. It's too vague. Don't you have any more specific suspects?'

'I can't think of any.'

'So it's no wonder the police settled on you so swiftly. Okay, what about the murder of Kōsaku Moro then? Anyone with a grudge against him?'

'Hmm, I can't think of anyone. I certainly can't imagine anyone, he wasn't really the guy to rub people the wrong way.'

'Girlfriend?'

'His?'

'Of course his. Who cares if you have a girlfriend now or not? Does he have a girlfriend?'

Ryūhei wouldn't admit it, but those veiled jabs Ukai occasionally slipped in packed quite a punch subconsciously.

'I don't think he was seeing anyone…' And then Ryūhei added one line as his form of revenge. 'Just like you.'

'…'

'Oh!'

Even from far away it was clear Ukai was hurt by that line. Ryūhei's attack had been too cruel for the single, divorced man. Ryūhei regretted his move a little. He needed the detective to help him out from now on. It wasn't wise to be hurting him now for trivial reasons.

5

Ukai rose slowly from his chair and announced that he wanted to have a look at the crime scene. He meant Flat 4 of White Wave Apartments, of course. Ryūhei couldn't believe his ears.

He had just managed to make his getaway from the place, and now the detective was saying they had to go back there? Ryūhei obviously didn't feel up to it at all, so if Ukai insisted on seeing the place, he would just tell him the address and have him go alone.

But the detective wouldn't back down. In fact, he insisted more strongly by referring to tradition.

'It's only natural that a detective would want to see the crime scene. And it's traditional for a Watson to accompany the detective willingly.'

'I'm Watson? I thought I was the client.'

'Leave logic out of it and come with me.'

What's a detective going to do without logic? Ryūhei frowned at Ukai's response.

'And you know the saying, right?'

Ukai was now also involving sayings.

'Which one?'

'The murderer always returns to the scene of the crime.'

Ryūhei sighed loudly. 'I told you, I'm not the killer! So why would I return to the scene of the crime?'

'Oh, that's right.' Ukai tried to calm his furious client. 'You want to learn the truth, don't you? If we're both there to make observations, we might learn something we wouldn't have learnt separately. And don't forget, once the police learn about the murder, we won't be able to take a look at the place any more. It's a chance we shouldn't let slip.'

'Do you have the slightest idea how to solve the murder? You seem so intent on going there...'

''Of course. That's why we need to go to Moro's place, so I can make sure.'

'...Are you sure you don't just want to take a look at a murder scene for the sake of it, as if you're a child?'

'Hu—huh, no, of course not!'

'I don't believe you. It doesn't sound as though you ever encountered a locked room murder before, either.'

'Of course not. That's only normal!'

'And that's why you want to go there, isn't it?'

'No! I'm not lying. I really don't care about experiencing a locked room murder myself, even one bit!'

Ukai was clearly irritated by the accusation.

'And while we may not have had the actual experience ourselves, you can't deny we have all experienced countless locked room murders. They may have all be "virtual" experiences, but the locked room mysteries our respected predecessors created are far more original and sophisticated than the real thing. They provide far better teaching.'

'You're talking about mystery novels, aren't you?'

'Of course. The numerous mystery novels I've read, and the countless locked room murders that occurred in those stories, have all become part of me. They whisper to me in my mind. They tell me that your locked room murder is simple. There's no need to make something difficult out of it. It's a simple trick that anyone with a love for mystery novels will see through. That's why I said I had an idea how to solve your locked room murder. But I need to see the place for myself to make sure. I'm certainly not just some disaster tourist who wants to take a look at a murder scene!'

'Oh, but how do you think it was done, then?'

'That I can't tell you now. I have to see the place myself first.'

Ryūhei wasn't left any option but to cooperate. The detective may be boastful, but perhaps he was actually very sharp. In the end, Ryūhei gave in and agreed to join Ukai on his trip to Moro's flat. It turns out that the client always returns to the crime scene as well.

Ryūhei and Ukai took the detective's own car, a Renault Lutecia. Even though his income was probably quite low, Ukai drove an imported French car. Ryūhei simply couldn't make out this man's sense of values, and how he ever planned for the future.

'Oh, sure, it's a Renault, but it's just a normal popular model. There's not much difference between it and a Civic or Corolla. Price is similar too.'

'So why not take a Civic or Corolla? They're less conspicuous.'

'Impossible.'

'Why?'

'Because I'm a private detective.' Ukai uttered those words as if they made sense. 'How can a private detective drive a regular, popular model produced here in Japan? You can't be serious. Listen, a detective's car is like their business card. Even if you don't invest in your office, you should never economise on your car. Their car is the one thing all private detectives take pride in.'

Aha. Ukai used the word "pride", but basically it was about keeping up appearances.

Once inside, Ryūhei was handed a worn-out baseball cap and a pair of light-brown sunglasses. He had to hide his face, even if just a little. Ryūhei thought it was better than nothing, so he put them on, but when he looked at himself in the rear mirror, the face that looked back was exactly like the face of someone on the run from the police. It had the reverse effect of what they were hoping for. But he still felt it was better than nothing if they needed to go through town, so Ryūhei kept them on.

'They suit you,' said Ukai, his eyes on the road. He probably meant it as a compliment. Or did he really think this suspicious look suited Ryūhei? Whatever his thoughts may be, Ryūhei and Ukai probably looked like a very dubious duo to other people. Imagine if a patrol officer should stop them to ask them some routine questions. No, wait, that's not even out of the realm of imagination, thought Ryūhei .

They parked the car in a street near Saiwaichō Park; the rest would be done on foot. The two of them walked side by side, pretending nothing was wrong at all. As they crossed Saiwaichō Park, Ukai turned to Ryūhei.

'You threw that plastic bag away in this park as you fled, I remember? Which garbage can was it?'

'Err, garbage can?' Ryūhei was taken aback, as he hadn't expected the detective would ask him about that. 'Err, that one over there.'

Ryūhei pointed at a rusty iron garbage can near the centre of the park. It looked more or less the same as when he had seen it a few hours ago. Plastic bags, plastic bottles, empty cans, old newspapers and other garbage had been thrown inside. In other words, a very ordinary garbage can.

Ukai jogged towards it and almost stuffed his head inside as he closely examined the contents.

'A bag from Hanaoka Liquors, was it? Hmm, I don't see it... I guess someone eagle-eyed must have taken it already.'

'Err, what are you doing?' Ryūhei timidly asked the detective, who seemed very focused on digging in the garbage.

Ukai looked up. 'I'm not digging in garbage.'

'It sure looks as though you're digging in garbage.'

Ukai sighed. 'You're really careless, you know.'

Ryūhei had no inkling of what Ukai was suggesting. 'What do you mean?'

'You don't see? I'm working hard to retrieve the evidence you threw away so carelessly.'

'Evidence?'

'Yes. But it appears it's gone now. Too bad. But it's unlikely the police have it.'

'What do you mean by evidence?'

'Think about it. You were drinking with Kōsaku Moro last night. I understand why you want to hide that fact, you wanted to make it appear as if you weren't in his flat last night. That's reasonable. But you went too far by disposing of the Hanaoka Liquors plastic bag, together with all the drinks and snacks. It was a very foolish act. Haven't you considered that it's a clearly established fact that Kōsaku Moro did actually go to Hanaoka Liquors last night to buy liquor and snacks and then went home? Once the police start their investigation, the owner of the liquor store or the employees there are sure to make a statement about it. It will only make the police curious if they don't come across the liquor and snacks in Moro's flat. And you threw it all in a bag and dumped it in a garbage can in the park. That's why I'm looking for the bag. But it seems as though it's gone already. Guess the homeless around here must have fished it out. Half-full bottles of sake and some unopened snacks must have seemed like treasure to them. Nothing to be done about it now.'

'....'

Ukai was of course absolutely right. Ryūhei's attempt at erasing all signs pointing to his presence in fact had the reverse effect. It was too late now, but Ryūhei gravely regretted his foolishness.

At the same time, Ryūhei was surprised by the abilities of Morio Ukai, who had noticed such a minor point just by listening to his story. Perhaps he had gone to the right person for help after all.

Next, Ryūhei and Ukai entered the grounds of White Wave Apartments. Nothing out of the ordinary could be detected from the surroundings. Bicycles in the bicycle parking rack, newspapers in the newspaper mailbox, clothes hanging from the clothesline. An absolutely normal sight. Nobody would ever suspect there was a man lying dead in his bathroom here.

'Did you lock the front door?'

'No, I only closed it behind me.'

'Well then, we can let ourselves inside. Come on.'

Ryūhei wasn't planning to wait outside, of course. The duo first made sure nobody was looking before they quickly slipped inside Flat 4.

Ukai took out two pairs of white gloves from the pocket of his jacket and passed one pair to Ryūhei. It was a cautionary measure to make sure they wouldn't leave any more fingerprints. Ukai used his gloved hand to turn the button on the doorknob to lock it from the inside.

'All right. For now it'll only appear as if Kōsaku Moro went out on his free Saturday and isn't home yet. We'll be safe here for the moment.'

'So we'll just pretend we're not here if someone rings the bell.'

Ukai nodded vigorously. 'Of course. Let's have a look at the body now... Huh!'

'What's wrong?'

Ukai looked all around him as he replied: 'What's wrong? Did you leave all the lights on when you fled the place? Everything is on, from the entrance hall to the hallway and the bathroom. How careless, how incautious, and what a waste of electricity!'

Ukai seemed genuinely shocked at what he saw. But Ryūhei protested.

'No, wait. It's because of the power outage. There was a blackout when I ran away, so all the lights were off. I didn't think of that when I left.'

'In any case, it was very careless.'

'Well, I guess so. But don't you want to take a look at the body first?'

Ryūhei led the way to the bathroom. The dressing room, the washing machine, the clothes basket, everything was as he had left it that morning. Even the cold air there was the same.

'Is this the dressing room where you spent the night?'

'Yes.'

'Didn't you catch cold?'

'I feel fine. The body is on the other side of that door.'

Unhesitatingly, Ukai stepped forward and peered inside the tiled bathroom. Ryūhei, too, took a look from behind Ukai. The peculiar situation was the same as last night: Moro was lying cold on the floor, completely dressed. It was a sight nobody would want to see twice, but this was Ryūhei's third time: last night, this morning and now.

He had hoped to be more accustomed to it the third time, but no such luck. It was a sight that left him speechless, no matter how often he saw it. As in the previous times, he could feel his throat go dry and his knees tremble. To control such a trauma, and to be able to face the reality in front of them in a calm manner, required tremendous mental strength. Which, sadly enough, Ryūhei did not possess at that moment.

In comparison, Ukai was far calmer than Ryūhei. Perhaps he just didn't quite grasp the seriousness of what had happened. Be that as it may, Ukai was observing the body coldly and dispassionately, and showed not a single sign of being afraid of the corpse.

'Ah, yes, I see. It's exactly as you told me. He was stabbed in his right side, through his clothes. And the weapon, aha, this is it. Hmm, yes, rather sharp. Rather small though, and a bit thin for a knife. But the handle is quite large. Yes.'

The detective kept mumbling to himself and then followed with: 'Perfect for the job.'

'Perfect for what job?' asked Ryūhei anxiously, but there was no answer.

'Let's have a look at the home theatre now. Is it this way?'

Ryūhei's question had been ignored completely, as if he had been talking to himself.

It wouldn't help much to argue about that, so he followed Ukai into the home theatre.

Needless to say, everything was basically the same as last night. The only difference being that Ryūhei had got rid of the drinks and snacks.

The moment Ukai stepped inside the room, he was bowled over by the white screen and the awe-inspiring sight of all the AV equipment. That's how most people felt when they first visited the room.

'Wow, this is amazing. It's like a real film theatre here. I didn't expect it to be this well-made. I can't believe it.'

Ukai's reaction was the standard response.

'And it looks as though the room has been swept clean. Not a speck of dust. Everything looks shiny. Kōsaku Moro must have been a very tidy person. Oh, what's this?'

Ukai crouched down on the carpet and picked something up. It looked like a small shell. It looked like a fragment of something. Ryūhei wanted to know what it was, so he took a close look.

'Oh, that's just a pistachio shell.'

'Just...?' Ukai reacted strongly to Ryūhei's observation. 'Just a pistachio shell? I may very well have just saved you from imminent peril. A word of gratitude would be appreciated.'

Ryūhei didn't quite see the point Ukai was making and thought he was being overdramatic.

'What do you mean, saved by you?'

'I assume this pistachio shell was from your little gathering last night. One of the snacks Moro brought from Hanaoka Liquors, I assume?'

'Yes.'

'So either you or Moro ate those pistachios last night.'

'Of course.'

'So either your or Moro's fingerprints should be on this shell.'

'Ah, that's what you mean!'

'Suppose your fingerprints are on this shell, and the possibility is just fifty percent. If the police had found this shell, you'd be in an even worse situation. It would be proof you were here in this home theatre last night.'

It was exactly as Ukai pointed out. It was indeed a dangerous mistake.

Ukai put the pistachio shell in his jacket pocket. He turned around to face Ryūhei and ask him a favour.

'Can you go to the living room next door and slam on this wall from that side? I want to get an idea of just how thick these walls are.'

Ryūhei did as he was asked and found his way to the room next door. He banged on the connecting wall a few times and waited for some kind of response. But none came. He banged two more times with his fist on the wall, and then returned to the home theatre.

'And?'

'Did you really bang on this wall? You didn't go to the wrong wall?'

'Yes, I banged with my hands on this very wall several times. Didn't you hear ?'

'I didn't hear a thing. Hmmm.' Ukai looked impressed. 'That means that the isolation in this room was done very thoroughly. Perfect for the job.'

'Perfect for what job?'

'...Then I guess it's either the living room or kitchen,' the detective mumbled to himself as he rubbed his chin.

'...'

Ryūhei's question was once again ignored, like a pet rabbit in a schoolyard. Actually, even that rabbit got a bit more attention than he was getting.

With pent-up frustration, Ryūhei followed the detective into the living room.

Ukai scanned the room carefully and then started to crawl on all fours near the sofa, like a dog sniffing around. Ryūhei knew he had to be looking for some clue left by the murderer. He could also see from the look on the detective's face that he was experiencing difficulty.

Next, Ukai extended his hunting area to the kitchen. The floor there was also explored on all fours, but that hunt also proved fruitless.

After a few minutes, Ukai got up again with a puzzled look on his face. He brushed the dust from the knees of his trousers.

'No good, I can't find it. I guess this is not the place. The entrance perhaps.'

Third time's a charm, thought Ryūhei, as he asked the puzzled detective once again.

'Could you please explain what you're doing? What's perfect for the job, and what is it you can't find?'

This time, Ukai responded immediately.

'The weapon and that space are perfect for the job, but I can't find any bloodstains.'

'What do you mean?'

'Okay, let me explain it to you. Once you hear this, you'll understand I'm not just here because I'm interested in seeing a crime scene.'

6

Ukai sat down on the sofa in the living room. Calmly, he started to explain, almost as if he had forgotten they were at this very moment illegal trespassers.

'The problem we face is the door chain which was in place inside the entrance hall. Do you agree?'

Ryūhei reacted bluntly. 'So?'

'Just consider the matter. Can you lock or unlock a door chain or a similar lock from outside in some manner? No, the answer is that it's impossible. For a cylinder lock you only need a copy of the key, and a professional can probably open or lock one with a piece of metal wire. But that's not the case with a door chain.'

'Yes, I see that. So you mean to say this was a perfect locked room…'

'No, no, that's not what I mean. If anything, it's too perfect, and full of holes!'

'Huh?'

'The culprit could have been standing on their hands for all I care, but that still wouldn't have allowed them to lock the door chain from the outside. In other words: the person who locked the door chain *had* to be inside. There's no other explanation.'

'But that means that the person who locked the door was...'

'Exactly.' A satisfied smile appeared on Ukai's face.

'It was... me?'

'Are you an idiot?' Ukai didn't hesitate to call his ex-brother-in-law an idiot. 'Why would it be you? You'd remember if you had done that, wouldn't you? Even if you were drunk.'

'Err, please stay calm, no need to get all excited. Calling people idiots is really not nice.'

'Okay, okay. I just lost my temper because I hadn't expected such a silly suggestion from you. I guess you don't read mystery novels.'

'Mystery novels? No, not really. Not just mystery novels though, I hardly read anything printed.'

'And yet you're in college?' Ukai sighed loudly.

'Guess it's more important in some colleges than in mine.'

The only detective stories Ryūhei knew were mystery films. He had hardly read any of the original novels of all the Seishi Yokomizo, Seichō Matsumoto and Agatha Christie films he had seen. He liked the mystery genre, but not in the form of a book. The scope of Ryūhei's interest was entirely in films.

'But what about mystery novels?'

'There's this often-seen theory. It's almost silly how often you come across it, so I didn't feel like going through all the trouble of explaining it, but I guess you don't know it. Let me explain it especially for you, as you're unfamiliar with mystery novels. It's obvious that the person who locked the door chain was none other than the victim himself, Kōsaku Moro.'

'But he's the victim.'

'Doesn't matter. Fact is, it couldn't be anyone else. It's the theory they refer to as "internal bleeding inside a locked room".'

'Internal bleeding inside a locked room? What's that?'

'What is it? Hmm.' Ukai crossed his arms and looked back disappointedly at Ryūhei. 'I hadn't expected to be asked such a basic question. Well, okay. It's the obligation of a detective to explain everything. You're a film buff, I assume you have seen the classic *Proof of the Man*?'

'Of course. It's from before I was born, though.'

'...'

Ukai was at a loss for words, and his eyes seemed to float aimlessly. Ryūhei could see how his shoulders drooped listlessly.

'What's the matter?'

Ukai wasn't able to hide his shock. 'No, err, nothing. From before you were born, you say? Oh, I guess the film's already over a quarter of a century old now. Aha, I see. We're in the twenty-first century now. I guess I'll hear about it more often now. What scary times we live in.'

To Ryūhei, the division in two centuries was nothing but a divider in a continuous period of time. So there was nothing scary about it. But Ukai seemed to feel something bigger behind it. But let's leave his views on the twenty-first century for now.

'What about *Proof of the Man*?'

'Remember how the film starts with a young black man being stabbed in a park, and how he, seriously injured by the attack, attempts to stagger into a restaurant on the top floor of a hotel?'

'Yes, I remember. But he collapses and dies in the elevator, leaving only a few mysterious dying words.'

'Exactly!' exclaimed Ukai. 'The film wasn't exactly about "internal bleeding inside a locked room", but it was quite similar. Basically, when someone is stabbed with a very thin knife in the back or side, and the knife remains in the wound, the weapon will actually function as a kind of plug and stop the wound from bleeding. So even if it's a fatal wound, you can still walk around for a while. And you can use your hands as well, of course.'

'Huh.'

'But several conditions need to be met for this to occur, the most important being the shape of the weapon. Something like a big butcher's knife wouldn't work. The ideal weapon would be a sharp knife with a thin blade, or something like an ice pick. The wound itself is small, so the bleeding can be stopped. But the wound is still deep, so it can be a fatal wound. So, a smaller knife is better than a larger one. And if the handle is big, the handle can act as a plug if the blade of the knife is stabbed all the way into the victim.'

'Aha, so that's why you said it was perfect for the job.' Ryūhei nodded at Ukai's explanation, now finally understanding what he had been mumbling about.

'Yes, I was talking about the knife lying beside the body. It was as if the knife had been made especially to create such a locked room. The location of the wound was also perfect. It may be a small knife, but if someone had been stabbed directly in the heart with it, they wouldn't have been able to move, of course. And the bleeding would have been too heavy if they had been stabbed in the neck or in the stomach. For the "internal bleeding inside a locked room" situation to occur, you need to get stabbed in your back or your side. Moro's wound in his right side is a textbook example. Bleeding must have been very minimal. And he was stabbed through his clothes, so his clothes must have absorbed the little blood that did flow.'

Ukai continued his explanation of the mystery of the locked room.

'I imagine the murder of Kōsaku Moro must have occurred as follows. Last night, at half-past-ten, Moro left you in the home theatre to take a bath alone. However, just as he had turned the shower on and was about to undress, the murderer X appeared suddenly, holding a knife. At this moment, it doesn't matter whether X rang the bell to be let inside or whether X had sneaked inside earlier. Anyway, despite Moro's desperate attempt to fight off his assailant, X managed to stab Moro fatally in his right side with the knife. But Moro did not give up, and eventually managed to push X out of the front door. It's also possible that X wasn't chased away, but that they fled the scene on their own. In nay case, X was gone. At that time, the knife was still stuck in Moro's right side. So what did Moro do next? To make sure X wouldn't return to finish him off, Moro himself locked the door with the chain.'

Ryūhei nodded. 'Aha! But his body was lying in the bathroom.'

'Yes. After he locked the door, Moro must have made his way back to the bathroom in a dazed state. And there he pulled the knife out of his side. But that only worsened the bleeding, and he lost his life. Thirty minutes after this happened, at eleven o'clock, you discovered Moro's body. And that's why the door chain was locked on the inside and you found Kōsaku Moro's body lying in the bathroom. And why you were alone inside the flat.'

'I get it now.' Ryūhei nodded vigorously. He was impressed by Ukai's deductions and it even made him feel slightly relieved. But he still had questions. 'But why did he go to the bathroom, instead of coming to me for help? If he had come to me, I could have called an ambulance.'

Ukai patiently continued his long explanation. 'It was probably an unconscious act on his part. You can assume that he wasn't able to think logically anymore whilst suffering from that severe wound. So what was on his mind then? It's simple. He was going to take a shower when he was suddenly stabbed. So even after he was stabbed, he was going to take his shower. So what controlled his actions at that moment, was the intention of taking a shower before he was suddenly attacked. It might seem senseless, but it's only natural that you start to act confused under such extreme circumstances.'

The explanation was sound and convincing.

'That's all I have to say about the possibility of bleeding inside a locked room. Anyway, things are clear now. There remains the matter of where the victim was stabbed. It's most likely the crime was committed in the living room or the kitchen. But you were in the home theatre, right in the next room. So there was the question of how a murder could have been committed in the living room without you ever noticing a thing.'

'So that's why I had to bang on the wall?'

'Yes. And the conclusion was that while the living room and home theatre are right next to each other, you can consider them completely different spaces. You could hold a sports tournament in the living room without someone in the home theatre ever noticing. So, the murder could easily have occurred right here in this room.'

'So that's why you went sniffing around here.'

'Yes. Whilst Moro was bleeding internally, I thought that at least some blood must have dropped on the floor here. But I couldn't find any stains. I even searched the kitchen, but nothing. I could have missed a stain of course, or the wound could really have been sealed off perfectly, and not one single drop of blood made it to the floor. Nothing we can do about it.'

'So the murderer stabbed Moro, either in the living room or the kitchen, and then fled through the front door. Moro then locked the door chain even though he was still wounded, and thus created the locked room situation. And then he collapsed in the bathroom. But, err, I have a question.'

'Yes?'

'Do you think the police will buy this? Will they believe I'm innocent?'

'Well, no, I'm afraid that it won't be that easy. The police aren't likely to simply accept our story. Even if they admit the possibility of Moro having bled to death after locking himself in, it still wouldn't prove that you were innocent. You'd still remain a very likely suspect in their eyes.'

'So what's the purpose of working out this locked room, then?'

'Humph, you think there's no meaning to that?' Ukai became sulky and pouted, but still continued talking.

'I only proposed a very viable hypothesis because you kept going on about locked rooms and mysteries and impossible crimes. If you think that my hypothesis has no meaning, well then, that's only because the locked room itself was not of any consequence in the first place.'

'Do you mean that the locked room isn't one of my problems?'

Ukai tilted his head. 'To be honest, I don't know yet. But what I can tell you is that finding some way to save you will be far more difficult than finding the solution to the locked room.'

7

Their conversation stopped for a while. And, as if it had been waiting for them, there was suddenly a loud explosive sound outside. They instantly recognised it as the noise of a motorcycle revving up. Ryūhei remembered he was already familiar with the sound, which was that of a motorcycle which would occasionally misfire.

'That noise…'

'Sounds as though something's wrong with the motorcycle.'

'I heard it last night too. Yes, after I left the home theatre at eleven and found the body in the bathroom, I heard that noise outside. I remembered I felt a bit annoyed by it, because who would keep on checking their motorcycle that late?'

'Aha, that means that the owner of the bike must have been outside working on it before eleven o'clock. How interesting.'

'Yes, if your idea is correct, they could actually have seen the culprit fleeing the flat.'

'That's very possible. Okay, let's ask them some questions. But before we do…'

The detective then proceeded to do something odd. He stood before the mirror above the sink, took out what appeared to be a make-up set from his pocket and started working on his face.

'I use this pen to blur my eyebrows… draw some wrinkles at the corner of my eyes… Hide the gloss of my skin to make it look rough…'

Ryūhei stared at the man as Ukai's face turned older in the mirror. The finishing touch consisted of a pair of green, square glasses and a flat cap. (He even had that in his pocket!)

'Tada, don't I look like a middle-aged police detective now? I was going for the look of No. 4 of the classic police drama *Seven Detectives*.'

'Ah, yes! You look exactly like a detective! I wouldn't be able to tell the difference between No. 4 and No. 5 though.'

'Let's ask our questions then. You just stay quiet and it'll be all right.'

Ukai and Ryūhei left Flat 4 via the front door. They looked around, but didn't see anyon working on a bike. The noise came from a bit further away, from the residents-only parking lot just beside the White Wave Apartments building. The two followed the noise.

A broken motorcycle was standing there, and a person who was obviously struggling with it. The machine was visibly old, but the person was young. And a woman. She was wearing a denim shirt and jeans. A blouse was lying on the concrete, presumably hers. She was still feeling hot though, as beads of perspiration were visible on her forehead. She seemed very determined to fix the machine. Even when the two approached her, the woman didn't seem to notice them and remained in a crouched position, checking the engine.

'Err, excuse us.'

She finally looked up when Ukai addressed her. Her eyes quickly moved to check them out in a very cautious manner. She probably thought them to be a very suspicious duo. Naturally.

'And who are you?' She sounded quite fearless. 'Sir, what business do you have with me?'

'Sir? I'm not that aged… oh, yes, I am.'

Ukai had forgotten he had disguised himself to appear older. What a waste of his disguising skills if he had given it all away like that! He hadn't expected a woman who looked somewhat similar in age to address him so distantly. But he somehow managed to go on, and took out a notebook with a black cover from his inner jacket pocket.

'This is my ID.'

Ryūhei was quaking in his boots as he stood beside Ukai. He almost cried out loud when he saw Ukai brazenly waving his fake police ID around. No way this was going to work. It was impulsive, imprudent, impossible!

'Oh, you're from the police. Is it about that college student who fell to her death last night?'

The woman was surprisingly easily fooled. She didn't even think of reading what was written on the cover of the notebook. It clearly said in golden lettering: Lucky Notebook.

'Yes, it's exactly as you guessed. We are investigating that incident. My name is Nakamura.'

As Ukai gave his fake name, he returned his notebook to his inner pocket. Ryūhei gave a silent sigh of relief.

'My name is Akemi Ninomiya. Who's that?'

The woman who called herself Akemi was of course looking at Ryūhei.

'Oh, he is Takeshita. Still a rookie, hahaha.'

Apparently Ryūhei had now been cast to play the role of a rookie detective. And for some reason he now had the name Takeshita. Ryūhei was absolutely trembling. He nodded clumsily at Akemi and hid meekly behind Ukai.

Akemi obviously seemed suspicious of Ryūhei. 'Hmmm, are there really police detectives who walk around wearing a cap, blouse and sunglasses? I thought they only existed in television shows.'

'They are quite rare indeed, hahaha!' Ukai decided to go along with Akemi as he laughed out loud. Ryūhei meanwhile was offended by that remark: it was Ukai who had dressed him like that!

'And what did you want to ask me?'

'Were you working on your motorcycle here around eleven o'clock last night as well? We have received information that someone heard the noise of a motorcycle engine around that time.'

'Yes, I was working on my bike. Still am.'

'Trouble with the engine?'

'I don't know what's wrong with it. But that's fine, I just like fiddling around. But so what if I was working on my bike here last night?'

'Perhaps you happened to spot a suspicious person then? By the way, from when until when were you here in this parking lot?'

'I first watched the nine o'clock television drama, so I think I was here from just after ten o'clock until eleven-thirty.'

'Long hours. Did nobody from the neighbourhood complain?'

'Surprisingly, no. I also don't think it was that loud.'

'All right. And you were working at this exact spot?'

'More or less.'

'And if you were to be exact?'

'I was working beneath the lights of the entrance gate. I had parked my bike there, in front of the gate. The lighting is better there.'

Akemi pointed with her right hand at a light on top of one of the posts of the entrance gate shared by the flats and the parking lot. So, last night, she had been working there on her bike from shortly after ten until eleven-thirty. Her testimony was therefore of great importance. The look on Ukai's face turned serious.

'You were standing there, at the gate?'

'Yes,'

'So you would have had a clear view of anyone entering or leaving any of the flats on the ground floor?'

The position offered a clear view of the four front doors of the ground floor flats. The closest one was the dreaded Flat 4, with Flats 3, 2 and 1 as its neighbours.

'I wasn't keeping an eye on them or anything.'

'But if someone had gone in or out of those flats, you would have noticed them, wouldn't you?'

'I suppose so.'

'And any person leaving those flats would also have to pass through this gate to leave the grounds, is that right?'

'Yes. But why do you want to know?'

'Please think carefully and see if you can remember. Whilst you were here between ten and eleven-thirty last night, did you see anyone? Anyone going through this gate and entering one of those flats?'

'Yes, I did.'

'You did! Who?'

'Mr. Moro.'

'Mr. Moro? And who might this Mr. Moro be?'

Ryūhei had to stifle his reaction to the detective's overacted fake question as he awaited the answer.

'He lives in No. 4. I think he's around twenty-five years old. Works at some film production company.'

'Aha. And when did he pass through the gate?'

'Right after I started working on my bike, so probably around ten o'clock. He went out through this gate and returned about fifteen minutes later.'

'And would you happen to know where he went?'

Ukai of course knew the answer already, but he still played the fool.

'He went to the liquor store.'

'How do you know?'

'Because he told me. As he went out, he greeted me and said he was just going to the liquor store.'

'Couldn't be any clearer. What about when he came back? Did he greet you again?'

'No, he just passed by without saying a word. He was holding something in his right hand. It was too dark to make it out clearly, but it was probably a bag from the liquor store.'

'And did you see anyone besides Mr. Moro?'

'Hmm, I don't think so.'

'Please think about this carefully. For example, did something happen at ten-thirty?'

Ukai was asking his questions rather bluntly now. Ryūhei's testimony had fixed the time of the crime within the thirty-minute period between ten-thirty and eleven o'clock. But the fact the victim was murdered whilst still dressed suggested it had happened right before he took his shower. So Ukai had determined the murder had to have happened closer to ten-thirty. And naturally, the murderer must have entered White Wave Apartments just before the murder, and exited the complex again right after.

'Ten-thirty? Ah!' Akemi suddenly looked up, as if she had recalled something. 'Now you mention it, I think I did hear a loud noise. At ten-thirty.'

'A loud noise? Where?'

'I think it came from Flat 4. It was a low, loud bang. You see that tilting bathroom window there?'

The bathroom window was right next to the front door.

'I think the sound came from there. For a moment I thought perhaps something had happened there, but nothing followed, so I didn't think anything more of it.'

'A—and you're sure this happened around ten-thirty?'

'I checked my wristwatch, so I'm sure. It was at ten thirty-five to be exact.'

'Aha. Excuse me for a moment.'

Ukai turned around to face Ryūhei and grab him by the shoulders.

'Hey, we couldn't have wished for anything better! Ten thirty-five at night. We can assume that was the time of the murder. She must have heard Moro falling on the tiled floor in the bathroom.'

'Yes, I think so too. If your theory is right, that means the murderer must have left the flat just before that.'

'O—of course I'm right.'

With absolutely confidence in his hypothesis, Ukai turned around to Akemi to ask his final question.

'Someone must have left Flat 4 just before you heard that noise at ten thirty-five. Did you see them?'

'No, there was nobody.'

'No... really?' The unexpected reply made Ukai feel a bit nervous. 'You didn't see anyone leave or enter the flat?'

'I'm sure. I was here the whole time, so I would definitely have noticed. Nobody passed by here except for Mr. Moro at ten o'clock and at ten-fifteen. And I was here the whooooooole time, until eleven-thirty.'

'But that's....'

Ukai crossed his arms faced with this conundrum. Ryūhei copied the posture as he also thought about the matter. Apparently, the only person who had passed through the gate around the time of the murder had been the victim himself. So where had the murderer come from, and how did they escape?

They hadn't made any progress in solving the locked room mystery, just made it more mysterious.

8

At this point it's about time for our two police detectives to make their appearance once again.

Readers in general are often forgetful and get easily bored. That's not just the case with readers of mystery fiction. The reading public in general is also very indifferent, so if a character doesn't appear for a long time, they tend to think of these characters as "people of the past", no matter how important their role in the story actually is. So now we have to spend a few pages with these detectives to make sure they don't have to suffer from such a cold attitude from the readers.

Some of the following scenes have already been described from Ryūhei's perspective, but please bear with me.

Previously, we saw how Chief Inspector Sunagawa and his subordinate Shiki discovered a bloodstain in the flat where Yuki Konno had been murdered. What happened next will be briefly summarised. For, whilst a police investigation might look flashy in television dramas, actual investigations are very boring and tedious. A detailed explanation hardly makes for an entertaining story.

It is a repetition of the same boring cycle: detectives finding a notebook in one of the drawers, but, on looking inside, all they discover is that the victim's handwriting was really bad; detectives getting hopeful when they find some magazine clippings, only to discover they were just cuttings from a mail order catalogue; detectives thinking they finally have something when they stumble upon a photograph, only to find a Dachshund smiling at them when they turn it around .

It's almost as if they are rummaging through a garbage can, checking what could still be eaten and what couldn't. The starting point of the investigation that commenced after sunrise was based on the information they had gathered that "could still be eaten".

The two detectives' task for the moment was to check up on the ex-boyfriend of the victim and see what he had to tell them.

The name of the ex was Ryūhei Tomura. Yuki's diary had revealed to the detectives how, early this year, Yuki and Ryūhei had an argument about his employment and how the two had an enormous fight in the college café in the middle of the day. Shiki and the others saw this as very vital information and soon their attention was focused on this Tomura.

'*Cherchez la femme*, as they say.'

'I don't know what you mean,' said Sunagawa.

'If a woman is killed, there's bound to be a man behind it.'

'Really? I have a feeling your interpretation is rather creative.'

But that didn't change the fact that their first goal was to locate Ryūhei Tomura.

They went to his flat first thing in the morning, but he was not there. Of course, it was only natural for them not to find the person they were looking for right away. Any detective knew that.

They asked a fellow college student who lived nearby and learnt that Ryūhei had probably not come home the previous night. If he had been home, he would have switched the television or stereo on loudly, and would have let out drunken howls. They would definitely have known if Ryūhei had been there.

Shiki immediately became convinced that Ryūhei was a neighbour with a bad attitude, an impression which only strengthened his suspicions against him.

The detectives learned the name of a friend of Ryūhei: Yūji Makita. They visited him at ten o'clock that morning. Makita seemed like a clever guy and seemed to instantly understand the reason the detectives were visiting him. He was very cooperative and immediately let them inside to question him. Shiki praised him in his mind as a model civilian.

Shiki asked Makita about Ryūhei's character, and he reluctantly recounted a certain episode.

'So, a few days ago, he had a bit too much to drink, and he started hugging a sign at the bus stop in front of the station. He was screaming things you usually don't say in front of other people....'

'Such as ...??'

'Well, basically, he was insulting his ex, Yuki Konno. In err, let's call it Japanese slang.'

'Aha!' Shiki let out a contented grunt. His profiling had been correct. It was clear Ryūhei Tomura not only had a bad attitude, but was also a man of bad character. And wasn't it clear from that episode that Tomura held a grudge against Yuki Konno? Shiki's animosity against Tomura only strengthened.

The detectives also learnt the name of the private detective Morio Ukai from Makita. The man was Tomura's brother-in-law.

If Ukai had only been a relative, this piece of information would not have attracted much attention, but his occupation of "private detective" made things different. Shiki was convinced the whole business reeked, and they quickly made their way to Ukai's office.

Sunagawa was either not able to keep up with Shiki's go-getter attitude, or he had no intention of doing his best from the start: either way, Sunagawa said nothing and just accompanied Shiki.

The duo arrived at the Morio Ukai Detective Agency at around ten-thirty in the morning. As they parked their car in the parking lot next to the multi-tenant building behind the train station, Shiki noticed something out of place parked there: an imported car (a Renault?).

They went up to the second floor and saw the door decorated with a white sign. They rang the bell and the door opened slightly. Only part of the detective's face was visible from behind the door chain. He was visibly surprised that he was being paid a visit by two well-built men.

'Is Ryūhei Tomura here? Hiding him won't help him a bit.'

'Ryūhei is not present in this establishment at the moment. Are you gentleman perhaps loan sha—are you from a loan company?'

It was perhaps rude of the detective to think these policemen were debt collectors for a loan shark. But didn't that mean that Tomura was probably the type of person who might have debts with a loan shark? Whilst the private detective may not have had that intention, he had basically admitted the fact.

Shiki's mental image of Tomura was more or less complete now, and it was not a pretty one.

'We're not loan sharks. Here's my ID.'

Shiki pulled out his ID in the most impressive manner he could muster. The moment he was shown the ID, Ukai's attitude changed.

'Oooh, you're cops. I needn't have been so polite then.'

'Aha, I see, you're one of those people.'

Shiki was put on guard. This Ukai had a knack for getting on a person's wrong side. Usually you'd be more polite in front of a policeman, not less!

The two police detectives were led into the office, where they asked Ukai a few questions. At one point, someone (probably a client) telephoned the detective.

'Hello, the Morio Ukai Detective Agency here. Aaaaaaaaaah, aha, aah!'

What was that? It was almost as if he had hurt his jaw the moment he answered the phone, Shiki thought, but he didn't think anything more about it. The two policemen didn't learn anything of interest from Ukai, but neither did it appear as though he was hiding Tomura.

And that is how the whereabouts of Ryūhei Tomura managed to evade Shiki, despite his watchfulness. Ryūhei Tomura had been extremely fortunate.

So Chief Inspector Sunagawa and Shiki had to leave the Morio Ukai Detective Agency empty-handed. Their next step was to see a man called Kazuki Kuwata. Ryūhei Tomura was Yuki Konno's ex-boyfriend, but this Kazuki Kuwata was her current (or, rather, her most recent) boyfriend.

That was obvious from just one look in her schedule book. Up until halfway through January, Tomura's name had made up the bulk of the entries, but after that, it was mostly Kuwata's name. It confirmed the impression that she had already moved on to someone else.

It was necessary to look up Kuwata, to see whether he was involved in the murder of Yuki Konno or not.

They called him in advance and agreed they would meet him at his part-time job. He worked in the video rental shop Astro near the main entrance of the college. In front of the shop stood a weird-looking figure of Astro Boy, but it was debatable whether or not it had officially been sanctioned by Tezuka Productions.

The two detectives entered the premises and found only one person working there.

'I assume you're Kazuki Kuwata?' asked Sunagawa as he showed his ID.

The employee answered in the affirmative. Kazuki Kuwata was built like a sportsman, tall and broad-shouldered. But his face was not tanned. A tan isn't as popular nowadays. His smooth hair was dyed in a brown-tea hue, and he looked quite handsome. Sunagawa was instantly on his guard against this man. Shiki knew very well that Sunagawa had a unique mentality: he had an instinctive aversion to good-looking men.

Sunagawa fired a relentless barrage of questions at Kuwata, who answered them calmly.

'When did you start seeing each other?'

'Two months ago.'

'How did you come to know her?'

'We sat next to each other at a party.'

'Did you get on well?'

'Yes.'

'Did she behave any differently lately?'

'Not that I noticed.'

'Did you have a fight with her lately?'

'Just small fights.'

'You were only dating for two months, but I assume her murder must be quite a shock to you nevertheless.'

This was the one question that seemed to affect Kuwata.

'Of course! It's constantly on my mind here at work. I will go to her funeral service.'

'Do you know Ryūhei Tomura?'

Sunagawa brought out Tomura's name without warning, to see how Kuwata would react.

'Sure, I know him,' Kuwata replied, as if the question were completely normal. 'A friend from college. He was Yuki's previous boyfriend.'

'Huh, I hadn't expected you two to be friends. And does Tomura know you were seeing Yuki Konno?'

'That I don't know. It wasn't something I especially needed to tell him about.'

'It appears that Ryūhei Tomura held a grudge against Yuki. Any thoughts on that?'

'He was dumped, so I doubt he was happy, but I can't say whether he would hold a grudge strong enough to want to kill her.'

'When did you last see him?'

'Yesterday.'

'Eh!' Even an experienced detective like Sunagawa couldn't hide his surprise. 'Yesterday? At what time? And where did you see him?''

'He came here to the shop. I think it was around five o'clock in the afternoon.'

'Why did he come here? Did he have something to discuss with you?'

'No. He came here as a customer. He rented a video.'

'A video? What video?'

'A mystery film called *Massacre Manor*. Perhaps you've heard of it?'

'Yes, I know it. It's a pretty old film. What a boring waste of time. I saw it in the theatres, I thought I was going to die there.'

Shiki interrupted them.

'Yes, I agree. Some friends and I rented the video when we were in college. Everybody hated it.'

'I advised him to get something else instead, but he insisted on that film for some reason, and he left with it.'

'Why did he insist on renting that film?'

'I guess he was going to watch it with someone else.'

'Aha… but that's odd.'

Sunagawa suddenly started to mutter to himself as he fell into deep thought.

'Ryūhei Tomura did not return home last night. Yet he came here to rent a video yesterday late afternoon. So where did he go with his video?'

Kuwata listened to the detective's mutterings and offered the answer.

'Probably to Mr. Moro's flat. Kōsaku Moro is an alumnus of our college. Tomura sometimes goes to his place to watch films with him.'

'Huh, Kōsaku Moro?'

This time it was Shiki who cried out in surprise.

After the duo of detectives learned that Kōsaku Moro lived in White Wave Apartments in Saiwaichō 5-chōme, they felt they were getting close. Saiwaichō 5-chōme was within a stone's throw of Takano Apartments, where Yuki Konno's death had occurred. There was a good possibility that Ryūhei Tomura had gone to Moro's place the night before with a rented video. To put it differently: it was very likely Ryūhei Tomura had been near the crime scene last night. This couldn't be mere coincidence.

'Ryūhei Tomura must be at Kōsaku Moro's flat. Or at least, had to be there last night. I'm sure we've got him now. Oh, and Shiki?'

Sunagawa suddenly turned to Shiki, who was in the driver's seat holding the steering wheel. He had a pressing question for his subordinate.

'You seemed to recognise the name Kōsaku Moro. Are you acquaintances?'

Shiki's eyes were fixed on the road leading to White Wave Apartments as he answered his superior's question.

'A friend from high school.'

'So our suspect happens to be a college junior of your old classmate. Small world.'

Shiki seemed to think for a while before he reacted.

'I guess so. It's really a small world. Chief Inspector, something odd happened last night.'

'What?'

'He—I mean, Kōsaku Moro— was near the crime scene last night, I think. I saw a man who looked very much like him amongst the crowd. It was only for a moment, but I'm fairly sure it was him.'

'So that fellow Moro was standing right there with us at the time? Could it be just a coincidence?'

'That I don't know. But he lives near Takano Apartments, so there's nothing strange about it if he happened to pass by there. But what was odd was....'

'Yes?'

'I'm not sure, but just as I was going to call out to him, the look on his face changed. As if he had been surprised by something he had not expected at all. He disappeared before I could call out to him.'

'Something he had not expected? Any ideas?'

'No, not at all.'

'Perhaps you used to bully him? Forced him to give up his lunch money to you? That's why he's still scared of you and fled.'

Stories about police officers who may represent justice now, but who used to be bad apples when they were younger, were far from rare. Sunagawa's guess was not completely unfounded.

'I never bullied him, I swear. Not him.'

'Aha, so you did bully others. Shaking people down for money, ordering them to buy your lunch for you or telling them to jump off somewhere.'

'Things of the past now, sir.'

Shiki admitted to (some of) the sins of his youth, just like that.

'But even so, there's no reason for him to be afraid of me now. We're both adults. Wow, look out!'

Shiki had to brake suddenly because a young man had suddenly jumped out onto the road in front of them. Sunagawa's head went back and forth like one of those drinking bird toys.

The young man wouldn't have looked out of place at the horse races: he was wearing a baseball cap and sunglasses. He was frozen in shock in the middle of the road, so it didn't appear as if he had intended to commit suicide by throwing himself in front of the car.

A nondescript middle-aged man in a suit sprang out from behind a nearby parked car (a Renault!) and pulled the young man onto the pavement.

'Damn yak, look where you're walking! Do you have a death wish!?'

'…'

Sunagawa was at a loss for words at Shiki's sudden outburst.

'Oh, err, sir, that was…'

'I know, you were a hooligan when you were younger,' declared Sunagawa. 'Anyway, stay calm and keep your eyes on the road when you're driving. We can't have a cop hitting someone with his car.'

'Yes, sir. I just got excited because you started digging into my past.'

'That wasn't my intention, of course.…'

'Anyway, forget about that. The question was: what did Moro see to give him such a shock? Perhaps it had to do with Yuki Konno's death. But we can simply ask him once we're there.'

'You're right.'

Shiki agreed completely with Sunagawa and once again focused on the road.

Needless to say, any hopes of the two detectives hearing the truth from Kōsaku Moro himself were doomed. They realised this fact soon afterwards, when they arrived at White Wave Apartments and discovered his body in the bathroom of Flat 4.

9

Ryūhei Tomura and Morio Ukai thanked Akemi Ninomiya for the valuable information she had offered them and left White Wave Apartments behind. If Akemi had secretly followed them, she would have witnessed a curious sight.

For as soon as the two "detectives" stepped outside the White Wave Apartments grounds, they walked hurriedly with their heads down, whilst carefully scanning their surroundings.

Which was clearly not the behaviour of police detectives, but more like fugitives.

But it was only natural the two of them would act like that. They had daringly returned to the scene of the crime and nearly solved the mystery by arriving at the theory of the "internal bleeding inside a locked room" when they found themselves stymied by Akemi Ninomiya's testimony. Not only Ryūhei, but even Ukai seemed to have lost all the confidence they had shown just minutes before.

'How could that be? If what she told us is true, your theory can't be right,' Ryūhei asked the detective aggressively as they walked along the pavement.

'We'll have to think about it later. Let's get back to the car first. We can't stay here, we could come across a cop at any moment.'

'You're the one who forced me to come.'

'Ahem.'

Ukai was naturally not happy with Ryūhei's remark, but he decided to remain silent. The fact that his theory had been blown to pieces had been a heavy blow to him. But still, considering the circumstances, wouldn't any mystery fan instinctively think of the theory of a seriously wounded person locking themselves in a locked room, even if it was an overused trope? Ukai had truly believed in his theory. The look on his face showed that he still simply couldn't believe he was wrong.

'Let's go over the events once again,' Ukai suggested, the moment they got into the car. Ryūhei of course had no reason to disagree. They started talking inside the parked vehicle.

'You watched *Massacre Manor* with Kōsaku Moro between seven-thirty and ten last night.'

'Yes.'

'It's possible the murderer crept into the flat whilst you two were watching your film? The front door probably wasn't locked.'

'Wait a second, why do you assume that's the case? That someone came inside whilst we were watching the film?'

'That has to be what happened. Remember what that woman said, what was her name again?'

'Akemi Ninomiya.'

'Yes, according to her, she started working on her bike at the front gate of White Wave Apartments from ten o'clock on. When Moro went out to Hanaoka Liquors just after ten, they greeted each other, and he also walked by her at ten-fifteen on his way back. But she didn't see anyone else. Doesn't that mean the culprit must have entered Flat 4 before ten o'clock in the evening?'

'I guess so. But the actual crime happened after ten-thirty. Based on what she told us, it's very likely the murder happened at ten thirty-five. That would mean the killer entered the flat before ten o'clock, but then waited for at least thirty minutes to commit the murder.'

'That would seem to be the case.'

'The culprit must be a rather patient person, then.'

'Perhaps they couldn't make up their mind?'

'But would someone who can't make up their mind sneak into someone's flat with a knife?'

'Perhaps the culprit is a very brazen person who can't make up their mind?'

'What kind of a person is that!?'

'How should I know? Perhaps they're not only someone who can't make up their mind while being brazen, but also a first-of-a-kind....'

Ryūhei wasn't going to push the matter any further. 'Oh, forget about it. Okay I get it, let's assume the culprit entered the flat before ten o'clock. And that the front door had not been locked.'

'Then our main problem is how the culprit escaped. Moro returned from Hanaoka Liquors at ten-fifteen. We know that from both your and Akemi's statements. You drank and chatted a bit with Moro, and he left the home theatre to take a shower around ten-thirty. We can assume that he was stabbed right after he left the home theatre. Akemi's statement that she heard a loud noise at ten thirty-five confirms that assumption. The murder probably occurred between ten-thirty and ten thirty-five.'

'I agree.'

'But we also have the mystery of the locked room, as the door chain was locked from the inside. The only explanation for that is, as I explained earlier, the theory that Moro himself locked the door whilst wounded.'

'So after the culprit fled, Moro locked the door chain, despite his fatal wound, and died afterwards.'

'Yes. So even if Moro died at ten thirty-five in the bathroom, the culprit would have left via the front door a few moments before.'

'However, Akemi Ninomiya did not see any such person.'

'Exactly.'

'She's even sure that nobody went through the front gate until eleven- thirty.'

'And thus my theory is killed!'

'Don't give up so easily! You just said it was the only possible explanation.'

'The past is the past, the present is the present. Akemi's statement changes everything. It's just as you said. Why would the murderer sneak inside before ten o'clock, but wait patiently until ten-thirty to commit the murder? You were right. The time of the culprit's flight would also make no sense. In order to flee the flat without being seen by Akemi, they would have needed to wait in Flat 4 until eleven-thirty.

But why would they need so desperately to avoid being seen? They could have just covered their face.'

'Hmm, that's true.'

'But suppose the culprit did wait until eleven-thirty, until Akemi stopped working on her motorcycle, and then left by the front gate. How then would they have locked the door chain? Moro would have been dead by then. And you say you didn't even look at the door chain until the following morning. I guess it couldn't have locked itself?'

'Impossible.'

'Of course it's impossible.'

'But where does that take us?'

'To the only possible conclusion.'

'Which is?'

'That you are the murderer.'

'Are you serious?' asked Ryūhei whilst making a ball of his fist, ready to hit Ukai if he said yes.

'No. It would make the case so much easier though. It would be the end of the whole mystery.'

As if the easy way out would be any comfort to him! Ryūhei punched Ukai. (Lightly.)

They had not succeeded in untangling the mystery of the locked room: they had only further confused the matter. Ryūhei realised they wouldn't be able to solve the murder at this rate, so he decided to address another significant aspect of the case.

Ryūhei turned to the detective, who was sitting behind the driver's seat, rubbing his face.

'Do you think there's a connection between Yuki's murder and Moro's last night?'

Ukai looked up sharply and placed his right hand lightly on the steering wheel.

'Oh, yes, that happened as well last night, didn't it? You were rambling on for so long about locked room this and locked room that, that I had completely forgotten about it. But that's exactly right, the locked room isn't the main problem. The main problem is that, in one single night, two important people in your life lost their lives, one after another, in curious ways. Yes, that dilemma is more important than your locked room. Perhaps it will be easier to solve the case by focusing on the connection between the two incidents.'

'So you believe there could actually be a connection between the two deaths?'

'Wouldn't that be the most natural assumption? It's hard to believe it was mere coincidence. They didn't just die on the same night, but don't forget that White Wave Apartments and Takano Apartments are only a one-minute walk from each other through Saiwaichō Park.'

'Did the same murderer kill them both, one after another?'

'That's quite possible.'

'I can't believe it. There's no connection between Moro and Yuki save for the fact I knew both of them. I don't even believe they ever met. So why would the murderer kill Yuki and then Moro on the same night? I can't imagine what the motive could be.'

'That I can't tell you right now. But I don't think you can be so sure there was no connection between Moro and Yuki.'

'How's that?'

'You told me yourself. Moro visited Hanaoka Liquors last night and came across the scene of Yuki's incident.'

'He only mingled with the crowd.'

'Perhaps. But I think that it's still an important connection. The real killer may have been amongst the crowd as well. We can even imagine that Moro might have seen something crucial amongst the crowd last night. For example, maybe he saw someone who shouldn't have been there, or something that didn't belong there.'

'And because of that, the killer suddenly set their sights on him too?'

An innocent bystander becoming the next target of a murderer because they happened to see something important. It's an often-seen plot twist in a series of murders. Only detectives with no resourcefulness would think of such a stale interpretation. Ukai was no exception.

'It's a possibility worth considering. A minor one, perhaps, but it's not unthinkable. Do you disagree?'

'I guess it's within the realm of possibility....'

'Okay then, let's start our investigation right away. What or whom did Kōsaku Moro see in front of Takano Apartments? That's our focus. Let's begin with Hanaoka Liquors.'

It was likely that there were still many police officers roaming near Takano Apartments, so if they parked in front of Hanaoka Liquors, there was a chance they'd get fined for illegal parking. So they had to walk.

The two of them stepped out of the car again and headed for Hanaoka Liquors.

'Waa!'

Ryūhei had just got out of the car and was trying to cross the street when he was almost hit by another car. Ukai quickly reached out and hauled Ryūhei back onto the pavement. The other driver, who had to stop his car, looked furious and was barking something at them. But then a middle-aged man in the passenger's seat said something, and the driver wilted and drove on as if nothing had happened.

'Man, I thought I was going to die,' said Ryūhei. It was indeed a very perilous moment, in more ways than one. But Ryūhei did not realise how dangerous it truly had been. The same holds for Ukai.

'Hey, be more careful. It would have been all over if you'd become involved in a traffic accident. Don't forget the police are looking desperately for you.'

Without realising that the police looking for Ryūhei had passed right in front of them, the two walked on. Perhaps ignorance is indeed bliss.

10

As they had expected, they spotted a police car parked in front of Takano Apartments. However, they did not see any uniformed officers around. The office worker who was crouching on the pavement whilst smoking might be a police detective, but once you start suspecting someone normal like him, you'll start to imagine that anyone on the street might be a detective.

Ryūhei tried to not look around too much. The two headed straight for Hanaoka Liquors and slipped inside.

It was dark inside the store, and completely devoid of customers. The store was open for business, but not doing any: the perfect circumstances. Ukai especially couldn't have wished for anything better. He flashed his Lucky Notebook in front of the owner, and it worked again. It was indeed a lucky notebook.

'Oh, thank you for your dedicated service,' said the owner politely, but it appeared as though his greeting was directed at the notebook, not his visitors. Such was the power of authority! Ryūhei had never felt this sensation before.

'Mind if we bother you with a few questions?'

'Now is perfectly fine, do ask.'

The owner's name was Ryōji Hanaoka, age fifty-three. He had a ruddy face, as if he himself had been drinking during the day. He seemed generally healthy, if a bit overweight. Ryūhei's first impression of the man was that he was the typical middle-aged male with a physique not suited to physical activity.

'White Wave Apartments, that old apartment complex is only about a minute walk from here, I believe? Do you happen to know a man called Kōsaku Moro who lives there? Twenty-five, wears glasses. Should be a customer here.'

'Yes, yes, of course I know him. One of my regulars.'

'Does he come often?'

'Yes, I'd say once every three days.'

'Aha.'

'Yes, yes.'

'One "yes" is enough, sir.'

'Ye—yes!'

Ryōji Hanaoka's voice suddenly jumped to falsetto as he straightened his posture. Just imagine how angry he'd be if he learnt they were fake cops. Ukai was going too far. He had a tendency to overdo things. It worried Ryūhei.

'And when did Mr. Moro last visit your establishment?'

'Yes. Last night.'

'What!' Ukai, of course, had to start with an overacted reaction. 'Mr. Moro came to this shop last night. What time was that?'

'Hmmm.' This was the first time the owner hadn't started with a "yes" first. 'He came here after the incident across the street, so… oh, yes, I remember. Just after ten o'clock. He arrived right after the ten o'clock music program started on the radio.'

'And his groceries were the same as usual?'

'Yes, he bought his usual things. Sake, *chūhai* cans, some snacks.'

'He paid cash?'

The detective's tactics involved mixing things up with meaningless questions.

'Yes.'

'Did you chat?'

'Not for long, but with what had happened across the street and all those police cars and onlookers gathered there, we talked a bit about that.'

'Could you be more detailed? What did you talk about?'

'Yes, oh, let me think.' The owner's eyes seemed to wander off as he searched his memory. 'He first said something about the crowd outside and asked me what had happened. So I told him it appeared someone had leapt to their death.'

'Aha. And then?'

'Yes, and then... I think that was it.'

'That was it? That was a really short conversation. You didn't talk about anything else?'

'No, he just said goodbye and left. That's all.'

'Hmm, that's all?' Ukai let out a low-sounding grunt. He couldn't think of a follow-up question.

'Did something happen to Mr. Moro? I thought the person who was killed at Takano Apartments was supposed to be a female college student?' asked Ryōji Hanaoka, appearing puzzled.

'Don't be too curious,' responded Ukai bluntly.

Of course, the owner's question had been the one the fake detective had feared the most. But if he flinched now, the owner would only become more suspicious. The detective knew that to make a lie stick, you had to act boldly. It was a smart move, but certainly not good for the heart.

'And you have to understand very clearly that everything we talked about here is vital information pertaining to the investigation. Do not repeat any of this to others, *capiche*?'

'O—of course, sir!'

It was lucky for the fake detective that the owner was the type of person who would buckle in the face of authority.

'By the way, did Mr. Moro go straight back home after he left here? Do you remember?'

'No, from what I saw, it appeared he walked in the direction of the crowd after he went outside. I was surprised, because at first it didn't seem as if he was interested in the suicide, but then he went to look for himself.'

'Aha. Did he perhaps meet or talk with someone in the crowd?'

'He did, he did.'

'What! Who, who was it?'

'I only saw it from a distance, but I think it was the owner of Kōreiken. That's the noodle restaurant over there.'

'A noodle restaurant? Hmm.'

Ukai's somewhat muted response came from the feeling that the occupation of owner of a noodle restaurant sounded too ordinary for a person whom they considered to be the key to a murder case.

In any case, they needed to learn Moro's movements of the night before, and it didn't matter whether the witness was the owner of a restaurant or a flooring craftsman. The two fake police detectives thanked the liquor store owner and left. The flashy Kōreiken sign was hanging about three shops down the street. Based on the name of the restaurant, they guessed that it served Korean-style noodle soup. The owner who appeared before them was obviously a hard worker. He was probably in his early thirties. Ryūhei theorized that he had once worked as an office employee, but had quit his job to start his own noodle restaurant.

'My name is Fumio Matsunaga. Thirty-three years old. I quit my job two years ago and opened this restaurant.'

His self-introduction was very methodical. Ryūhei's guess had been surprisingly accurate. Sadly, there were no prizes to be won.

'Just going to bother you for a moment, but we have a few questions.'

'Yes, of course.'

Fumio Matsunaga's "yes" was brisk and to-the-point. And he never repeated it.

'We just visited Hanaoka Liquors. We were told you were amongst the crowd in front of Takano Apartments last night.'

'Yes, I was there. I had just closed up. I think I was there between ten o'clock until ten-past. But why do you ask?'

'Did you see or talk with anyone whilst you were there? People you know.'

'I saw a few people I knew in the crowd, but I only spoke with one of them.'

'Aha, and this person was...?' Ukai asked in a nonchalant manner, but with a high degree of expectation.

'Mr. Moro. One of my regulars.'

The expression on Ukai's face relaxed when he heard the answer he had expected.

'I see. All right, a question about this Mr. Moro then. What did you talk about last night?'

'Nothing special. He said something like "Did she die? Poor thing", and I replied that it certainly looked that way.'

'And then?'

'And that was it.'

'And that was it? That was all?' The ball of expectations which had been growing inside of Ukai suddenly deflated like a balloon.

'Ah, but something odd did happen.'

The ball of expectations was being inflated again.

'And what did happen?'

'I don't know exactly myself actually. But Mr. Moro suddenly turned completely pale. Appeared to me as if he had seen something utterly surprising, something unbelievable.'

'Re—really!'

This was the moment Ryūhei and Ukai's baseless hopes turned into certainty. Kōsaku Moro *had* seen something in front of Takano Apartments last night.

'A—about what he saw. What did he see to give him such a surprise? Please tell us.'

'I don't really know, to be honest.'

'Please try to remember. Did he see some person he had not expected, or perhaps found something strange? We need to know.'

'But I really don't know.'

'I implore you to try and remember.'

'Err, detective?' Fumio Matsunaga suddenly cast a suspicious look at Ukai.

'Ye—yes, what's the matter?'

'Aren't you speaking differently from a moment ago? "Implore" and "please"... You sounded a lot blunter at first...'

'Eh! Ah! Ah!'

The shock rendered Ukai speechless for a moment. The restaurant owner was right. Until now, Ukai had played his role in an arrogant, overbearing manner, like the self-proclaimed No. 4 of *Seven Detectives*, but the moment the crucial statement reached his ears, he had reverted back to his usual self. Nothing good ever comes from being happy.

Ukai lost his composure and a large bead of perspiration appeared on his forehead.

But just as they thought the game was up....

Ryūhei suddenly cried out. 'What's that siren!?'

They didn't even have to make an effort to make out the noise. A loud siren was coming closer and closer. It was not the siren of a fire truck. Ukai quickly made use of the moment to return to his police persona.

'It appears something has happened. Takeshita, we have to go too.'

'Ta—Takeshita?' Ryūhei remembered that he was supposed to be Takeshita of the police. 'Yes, err, Chief Inspector, we'd better see what's the matter.'

Ryūhei immediately played the role. They had to leave the place immediately for more than one reason. Somehow, the two appeared to work best together whilst under pressure.

'We'll leave it at that. Thank you for your cooperation. Goodbye.'

Ukai quickly thanked the man and left the restaurant together with Ryūhei, leaving a confused Matsunaga behind.

Ukai wiped the perspiration from his brow. 'Phew, that was close. That man was sharp! I wonder what's beneath that façade of a noodle cook...'

'He's just a normal noodle cook!' Ryūhei said as he walked rapidly away from the place. 'I wonder what those sirens are?'

'Let's get back to the car first,' said Ukai as he looked straight ahead. 'At the very least, we know that there are police cars roaming around here.'

Ryūhei followed him in a dispirited manner. The noise of the sirens was only coming closer. Once in the car, they drove off without any clear destination. They went slowly, making sure not to go too fast. Naturally, they would have preferred to race away as quickly as they could, but that would only have attracted the attention of the police.

As they passed by the White Wave Apartments, Ukai suddenly spoke up tensely: 'Look over there. I knew it.'

He clicked his tongue and banged the steering wheel with his fist.

'They must have found the body in the bathroom. That was faster than I'd expected. I was hoping we'd have at least one night.'

Ryūhei looked out of the car window as Ukai spoke. A few police cars were stationed in the parking lot where they had been talking with Akemi Ninomiya. The red lights were revolving fast. There were both uniformed officers and plainclothes detectives. The onlookers had already formed a small crowd in front of the complex.

The car with Ukai and Ryūhei inside tiptoed its way slowly past the scene.

11

Now it's time to explain how the body in the bathroom of Flat 4 of White Wave Apartments was discovered by the police. The discovery was, of course, the work of our two police detectives... or that is what you would expect. But it was in fact the work of Akemi Ninomiya, to be exact. It happened as follows.

After Chief Inspector Sunagawa and Shiki had nearly run over Ryūhei Tomura, the very person they had been desperately looking for, they arrived safely at White Wave Apartments. When Sunagawa saw the exterior that displayed the name of the complex, Sunagawa muttered to himself: 'Looks like a shabby terraced house, like one of those traditional Japanese *nagaya*. I had expected something else.'

His rude opinion was shared by Shiki.

Since the two detectives had come by car, they naturally parked in an open spot in the apartment building parking lot. They noticed a young woman repairing her broken motorcycle there, but they paid her no special attention and headed straight for Flat 4.

They rang the bell a few times. There was, of course, no answer. But this time, the policemen were not about to leave just because there was no answer, for it was possible that Kōsaku Moro was hiding Ryūhei from the police.

But they couldn't just enter the flat either. They hadn't got a warrant, and there was no emergency situation at hand. With nothing else to do, Chief Inspector Sunagawa decided to ask some questions, just to kill time. His target was, of course, the woman who happened to be standing nearby: Akemi Ninomiya.

It would turn out to be a major prize for the police detectives. For as far as Akemi knew, this was the second time that day she'd been questioned by two men claiming to be from the police. No wonder she thought the visit was strange.

It was clear from both her behaviour and the look on her face that she did not trust the two men.

'Are you really from the police?'

Sunagawa answered in the affirmative as he nodded and showed his ID. He thought this would clear things up immediately, but to his surprise Akemi squinted at the ID.

'Is that thing real? Let me look inside.'

She snatched the police notebook with the ID from Sunagawa's hand and looked inside.

'Your handwriting is awful.'

'Hey, don't read that!'

'Hah, I couldn't, even if I wanted to,' snorted Akemi as she handed the notebook back.

'So the detectives who came earlier were your colleagues? Why do you keep coming here? Did something happen?'

The two policemen were shocked to hear this, of course. At first they thought that perhaps another team had also followed a lead to White Wave Apartments, but it didn't seem as though that was the case. They asked about the two "policemen" who had come earlier.

'One of them was Nakamura. Around forty, wore a plain suit, pair of awful glasses and a flat cap. The other was younger, wore sunglasses and a baseball cap.'

'A police detective who wears a baseball cap and sunglasses? Is there really such a person?' mumbled Shiki, who had completely forgotten his own outfit yesterday. Somewhere in his mind, he recalled seeing someone somewhere wearing a baseball cap and sunglasses, but had not thought any more about it.

'And what did those two men ask you?'

Akemi's answer to Chief Inspector Sunagawa was vague.

'Err, what was it again? I think they said they were investigating the fall at Takano Apartments, but for some reason, they kept asking me about Mr. Moro in Flat 4. Whether someone had entered or left Flat 4 at around ten-thirty last night. Stuff like that. I didn't really understand what they wanted to know.'

Chief Inspector Sunagawa and Shiki didn't understand the meaning either. But they didn't press the matter further, as they had other questions to ask.

'Do you know where Mr. Moro from Flat 4 is right now? We rang his bell, but there was no answer. Has he gone out? Or is he inside? It would be a great help if you knew,' Shiki asked her.

'Oh, but that can be answered easily enough. Just go inside and look.'

Sunagawa sighed and walked off, looking at the ground and shaking his head. The back of his suit seemed to shake too. If it could speak, it would have cried out: "Amateurs!"

'That's easier said than done,' Shiki tried to explain. 'Policemen can't simply enter somebody's home, not without a warrant, that is. They are quite strict about it.'

'What if I go inside and have a look then?'

'Eh! Well, err, but... Chief Inspector?'

'Hmm, well, but suppose the door's locked.'

The words coming out of the two policemen mouths may have appeared hesitant, but secretly both of them really hoped she could help them out. Akemi seemed to have sensed their secret wish, as she added: 'Oh, doesn't matter if it's locked. I've got a copy of the key.'

'A copy of the key?'

'Why?'

The policemen were baffled by this revelation. Akemi swelled with pride.

'I own the place. I might not look the part of a rich lady, but my family's pretty well off.'

Sunagawa repeated her words in utter amazement. 'You're the owner!?'

'Perhaps you would prefer to call me the landlord of a shabby terraced house?'

'...'

The self-proclaimed wealthy lady left the speechless policemen behind and disappeared into the building, only to reappear jangling a bunch of keys. It was the proof she was the landlord. They headed straight for Flat 4 and rang a few times at first to make sure there was no answer. She reached out for the door knob, but then exclaimed:

'But it's not locked at all. How silly.'

The door knob turned smoothly. Akemi pushed open the door and shouted out.

'Mr. Moro! It's me, your landlady Ninomiya! I'm coming in. Is that all right? Sorry to intrude!'

She kicked off her shoes and stepped inside. She may have called herself a rich lady, but her manners didn't reflect the finesse or class you would expect. Her audacity startled Chief Sunagawa and Shiki, but they were actually quite grateful and waited for her outside the door in silence. After a while Akemi came out of the room in the back. She shook her head at the police detectives.

'Nobody here. I guess he's gone out. Oh, wait. The bathroom door is open.'

Needless to say, Akemi could not have known what a horrible sight awaited her beyond the door. The police detectives had no inkling either of the imminent horror and waited for her.

Keen readers can probably guess what happened next. And what did actually happen will hardly disappoint them.

A few seconds passed after Akemi disappeared from the detectives' view, then an ear-splitting shriek reached the entrance hall. Sunagawa and Shiki looked at each other for a moment and quickly rushed inside. They entered the dressing room, where they found the once-perky Akemi crouching on the floor. Trembling, she pointed to the bathroom without saying a word. The detectives took a look inside. They found the body of a man in his twenties lying on the tile floor.

'What the...!' Shiki was rendered almost speechless by the sight.

Chief Inspector Sunagawa, on the other hand, tried calmly to ask Akemi a question.

'Is that Kōsaku Moro?'

Akemi, in a hoarse voice, barely managed to answer the question in the affirmative

A few minutes later, White Wave Apartments had become a noisy spot with police cars and onlookers. How strange it was to be confronted with almost the same scene yesterday and today, even if one occurred at night and the other during the day, Shiki thought to himself. As Shiki stood next to White Wave Apartments, looking out at the road, he saw a Renault pass by out of the corner of his eye. But, needless to say, he paid no special attention to it.

The two police detectives had been hunting frantically for Ryūhei Tomura, but they always just missed him.

As always, the police detectives had to go elsewhere until the crime scene investigators were done with their job. Sunagawa and Shiki didn't know what to do, so they ended up in the home theatre.

The moment Sunagawa stepped inside the special space, he exclaimed: 'Oh, this is a very impressive room. A private theatre? Aha, Kazuki Kuwata told us that Ryūhei Tomura would often visit Moro to watch films together, I guess he was telling the truth.'

'Does seem like that,' said Shiki as he checked the labels on the videotapes lined up on the shelves on the wall. 'I think we can assume that Tomura brought his video here last evening and watched it together with Moro in this very room.'

'Fuhahahahahaha!'

'What's so funny? And why are you faking your laugh?' Shiki asked, puzzled.

'Ahem, I wasn't faking. I was laughing because you said something funny, Shiki. You're too gullible!'

'How so?'

'That story of Ryūhei Tomura visiting Moro last night to watch a video together, that's what's fake. It's a fake alibi prepared by Tomura.'

'A fake alibi? A fake alibi for what?'

'The murder of Yuki Konno! What else?'

Sunagawa's accusation could be heard clearly in the small room. The Chief Inspector hardly had a golden voice, but the excellent acoustics of the room made him sound good. Sunagawa was in great spirits.

'The murder of Yuki Konno!' Smugly, Sunagawa repeated his words.

'Aha, I get what you're driving at. So Tomura decided he would kill Yuki Konno at Takano Apartments last night because she had dumped him. But he knew he'd become a suspect if he just killed her like that. The best way out was to prepare a fake alibi. So he asked someone close to become his accomplice: Kōsaku Moro.'

'Exactly. Tomura went to the rental shop Astro and rented *Massacre Manor,* right under Kazuki Kuwata's nose, so as to create the impression he was going to watch it with Kōsaku Moro. But that was not what happened. Last night, at nine forty-two, Tomura murdered Yuki Konno at Takano Apartments. When the investigators arrived on his trail, he planned to say he wasn't the murderer; that he had been watching a film with Moro that night and that we could check with Moro.'

'And Moro would of course have been instructed beforehand by Tomura. He would confirm that Tomura had been with him that night and that they watched a video together. So Tomura could claim he wasn't the murderer.'

'That's the gist of it.'

'So why has Moro been murdered, then?'

'Well, use your imagination. Tomura's criminal scheme went wrong. Nothing strange about that. They took the life of someone, so it's only natural they'd start to distrust each other.'

'So the accomplices had a falling-out?'

'Yes, that has to be it. I don't know what started it, but perhaps Kōsaku Moro was about to break his promise and come clean with the police.'

'Or perhaps Ryūhei Tomura decided he couldn't trust Moro after all.'

'Yes. Perhaps Kōsaku Moro turned from accomplice to blackmailer, now he had a hold on Ryūhei Tomura. Plenty of possible scenarios. But at any rate, having accomplices might sound nice, but it's not that simple. Once the trust is gone, murder is likely to follow.'

'I agree. Oh, but wait, I have a question, then.'

'Yes?'

'To do with what we talked about in the car. Moro was in the vicinity of Takano Apartments shortly after ten o'clock last night.'

'Ah yes, you said you saw him.'

'Yes. If Moro was Tomura's accomplice, what was he doing near Takano Apartments at that time? It was after the crime had already been committed and he'd know the police would be around.'

'Oh, that's easy. Don't they say "the murderer always returns to the scene of the crime"? Tomura must have wanted to know what was happening at Takano Apartments after he committed the murder. But he didn't want to actually return to the scene of the crime himself. So, he asked Moro to mingle with the crowd and have a look on his behalf. I imagine it was something like that. Or perhaps it was only when Moro saw all the commotion and the police officers at Takano Apartments for himself that he fully realised how grave the situation was. Scared, Moro returned to White Wave Apartments, and that's when they started to get into an argument...'

'Aha. So Tomura killed his unreliable accomplice and fled.'

'That would explain everything.'

No, not everything, Shiki thought to himself. Shiki couldn't forget about that mysterious look on Moro's face, that expression of utter shock he showed for a moment whilst he was standing in the crowd. Why did Moro look so distressed? It didn't look like the shock of realising how serious things had become. The expression on his face was more as if he had been hit by a thunderbolt.

But Shiki did not voice his doubts. Sunagawa's theory was sound, and his doubts were based on nothing more than his subjective impressions.

In any case, there was no doubt that Ryūhei Tomura was their killer. And wasn't that what they needed to know? Mentioning irrelevant matters would put Sunagawa in a bad mood. Which Shiki liked to avoid.

'That would mean that Ryūhei Tomura killed both Yuki Kanno and Kōsaku Moro. What an evil killer he must be, to kill two persons in one single night. We have to catch him quickly or else more victims might follow.'

'Yes. But the problem is we don't know where he fled to... Ah!'

'What's wrong, sir?'

'I almost forgot! Akemi Ninomiya mentioned it to us earlier. Two men who said they were from the police had asked her about Flat 4.'

'Oh, yes, I remember now. One of them was around forty, wearing a plain suit, glasses, and a flat cap. The other was younger, with a baseball cap and sunglasses.'

'A young man wearing a baseball cap and sunglasses. Shiki, don't you remember, didn't we see someone with a baseball cap and sunglasses today?'

'No—no way!' Shiki wore an expression of utter disbelief on his face. 'That fellow I almost ran over?'

'Yes. And I think his companion was a middle-aged man wearing a plain suit. I only saw them for a moment, and I didn't think too much about it then, but I'm fairly sure.'

'Those were the fake cops. Yes, that does sound likely. But why would they be hanging around the crime scene pretending to be from the police?'

'It's simple. The murderer always returns to the scene of the crime. He must have fled first, but then become worried again, so he came back. He might have left something here, or he wanted to wipe his fingerprints.'

'He might even have planned to wipe out any witnesses who could cause him trouble.'

'Yes, that's also possible. A murderer won't hesitate to commit more murders in order to hide one. Yes, they must have been Moro's killers.'

'So, one of those two men was Ryūhei Tomura?'

'Yes. Based on his age, I'd say that young man who wore that baseball cap so strangely had to be a disguised Tomura.'

'But who was that forty-ish man with him?'

'A man in his forties wearing a suit isn't much to go on. Damn, we should have paid more attention to those two!'

'Yes. Oh, but I do remember the car they drove, because it's not one you see very often. I'm sure it was a Renault. A medium-sized model called Renault Lutecia. Huh, but wait… I think… I think I saw it… somewhere.'

Chief Inspector Sunagawa grabbed Shiki vigorously by his shoulders. 'What's wrong? Batteries running low!?'

Shiki glared at his boss. He wasn't some kind of toy.

'No, I was talking about their car. It was a Renault, and I'm sure I saw it somewhere else recently. Ah!'

Shiki clapped his hands after much thought.

'I know! I remember, it was at Morio Ukai's place. There was an imported car in the parking lot next to the building where his agency is located. That was a Renault, too. Sir, it can't be a coincidence. There can't be many of those cars driving around in the city.'

Ryūhei Tomura was driving around in a Renault with a mysterious middle-aged man. A Renault had been seen in the parking lot in front of the office of Tomura's ex-brother-in-law Morio Ukai. It was only natural to connect the two facts.

Chief Inspector Sunagawa nodded a few times. 'I get it. The forty-ish man accompanying Ryūhei Tomura was Morio Ukai. But wait, he's only in his thirties….'

'He must have disguised himself. You can easily add ten years or so with make-up. And the glasses and flat cap helped make him look a bit older. It has to be Ukai.'

'Aha. Damn, pretending to us as if he had nothing to do with it whilst he was secretly working together with Tomura. Making fun of us?'

Shiki felt humiliated as well. 'I should have run him over.'

'Err, no, it was probably better you didn't.'

'I wouldn't have killed them.'

'Then it's all right. Next time perhaps.'

The comfortable feeling knowing that nobody was around listening to them led to a rather extreme conversation. They were half-joking, of course. But also half-serious. At that moment the door of the home theatre flew open, as if to stop their highly unprofessional chat. A uniformed officer stuck his head in the door. It was Patrol Officer Katō, whom they had met the evening before.

'Chief Inspector Sunagawa, the C.S.I. team have finished their work. You may enter the crime scene.'

'Ah, okay, thanks.'

Sunagawa's salute back always looked characteristically clumsy.

'Patrol Officer Katō.'

'Yes, sir?'

'You didn't overhear us talking right now, did you? No, okay, that's fine. Lead us to the body then.'

12

There is no need to offer a detailed account of the body of Kōsaku Moro which had finally been found by the police.

The police detectives were looking at the same horrible, shocking sight that had caused Ryūhei to faint the night before. More than half a day had passed since then, of course, but the medical examiner's inspection had been accurate.

'Estimated time of death is the two-hour period between nine-thirty last night until eleven-thirty. I might be able to narrow it down even more if I cut him open, but you can start with that.'

'Cause of death?' asked Sunagawa.

'He was stabbed with a thin blade in his right side. There are no other exterior wounds. So this wound here was the fatal one. It's likely that the direct cause of death was shock due to blood loss.'

'Sir, this knife was lying at the scene.' Shiki showed a knife sealed inside a plastic bag to his boss. It was a knife with a thin, sharp blade, confirming the words of the medical examiner.

'Can we assume this was the murder weapon?' Sunagawa asked the medical officer, not daring to be too decisive.

'It matches the wound.'

That was all he said. There was a nuance to his words that implied it was not the job of a medical examiner to determine the murder weapon. Sunagawa decided to change his question.

'Does this thin knife match the wound in Yuki Konno's back, then? The woman who was killed last night.'

'I can't be absolutely certain,' the medical examiner declared. 'But it's true that the wound in this man's side and the wound in the back of the woman who died last night are very similar. It's very possible that both wounds were made by the same weapon.'

Whilst the medical examiner had chosen his words very carefully, they did help confirm Chief Inspector Sunagawa's interpretation of the case.

Holding that knife in his hands, Ryūhei Tomura had first committed a murder in a room in Takano Apartments, and then another murder in a bathroom in White Wave Apartments. Twice he had done his vile deed. The thought made Shiki shudder.

It was a bold crime. The perpetrator had left the murder weapon at the crime scene, almost as if he were showing off. Had there been no reason for him to get rid of the weapon? Shiki stared silently at the bloody knife that had been left at the scene.

It was more than likely that this knife was truly the murder weapon. It would have been a great piece of evidence if Ryūhei Tomura's fingerprints had been on it, but nowadays murderers know better than to leave their prints. It was also obvious from one look that this was an ordinary knife, and it would be difficult to trace where it came from. Shiki's instinct told him it would be hopeless to even try identifying the murderer through the murder weapon.

Speaking of fingerprints, they had been found not only in the bathroom, but in various places, from the entrance hall and kitchen to the home theatre. But even if some of those prints belonged to Ryūhei Tomura, they wouldn't be of much help. He was a friend of Moro, so there'd be nothing odd about his fingerprints being found in Moro's place. That was a dead end too.

Chief Inspector Sunagawa started muttering to himself: 'We can expect more from witnesses than from the evidence. At the moment, we only have the hypothesis that Ryūhei Tomura visited this place last night. We have the information we learned from Kazuki Kuwata at the rental shop, and we've also got a witness from whom we learned that someone who might be Tomura, accompanied by Morio Ukai, has been roaming around the neighbourhood.'

'Yes, the two we almost ran over… err, I mean, the two we saw.'

'So if we can find someone who actually saw Tomura visiting this flat, then we have a proper case against him. It would be even better if someone witnessed Tomura leaving Moro's flat in the period between nine-thirty and eleven-thirty last night.'

'A witness at those hours?'

'Let's hope that little lady has something for us. I had the feeling she had more to tell us.'

Chief Inspector Sunagawa and Shiki spoke with Akemi Ninomiya again. She was sitting on the sofa in the living room. She seemed to have recovered from her initial shock and had regained her complexion. They asked her about last night, and she replied that she had been working on her motorcycle at the front gate.

Naturally, the police detectives were very pleased to have found the very witness they had been looking for.

'We want to know whether anyone left this flat last night? The time was...'

'Around ten-thirty, wasn't it?'

'Err, yes, around that time.' Sunagawa was slightly surprised that she knew the time. 'Between nine-thirty and eleven-thirty. So that would make it around ten-thirty. Ho—how did you know?'

'Those police detectives earlier, I mean, those fake detectives, they asked me the same thing.'

'Aha. And what was your answer?'

'I only saw Mr. Moro last night. He left his flat at ten o'clock, and returned about fifteen minutes later. I didn't see anyone else.'

'What! So Mr. Moro was alive until at least ten-fifteen?'

'Yes. That I can guarantee.'

'So that narrows his time of death down to the period between ten-fifteen and eleven-thirty. That's fantastic. Did you see or hear anything else out of the ordinary?'

'There was a loud noise from Flat 4's bathroom at ten thirty-five. Like someone collapsing on the floor.'

'What! At ten thirty-five! That must have been when Mr. Moro died.'

'Those fake police detectives said the exact same thing. Tell me, were those two really fake detectives?'

Sunagawa was lost in thought, so Shiki answered instead.

'They were genuine, authentic fake detectives. They may even be the people who murdered Mr. Moro. You might have been in danger.'

'How's that?'

116

'It's likely they were looking for witnesses. Their goal was, of course, not to find the killer. It was the opposite. They probably planned to find and eliminate any witnesses, in order to escape the clutches of justice. But fortunately, you only heard a noise and didn't see the murderer, is that right?'

'Yes, I didn't see the killer.'

'That's why you're still alive. If you had seen the murderer and told those two, by now you'd have been...'

'I'd have been....?'

'This perhaps.'

Shiki pretended to strangle himself. Those two might have eliminated you like *this*, Shiki's pose was supposed to convey. But Akemi Ninomiya didn't seem to grasp the seriousness of what could have happened. She was laughing heartily at the sight of Shiki.

'Really? Those two didn't look like bad people, you know.'

If Ryūhei Tomura in his utterly desperate situation had heard her say those words, he would have cried out in gratitude. Shiki, however, was not going to reconsider his image of "the evil multiple murderer Ryūhei Tomura" so easily.

'You shouldn't judge people by their appearance,' said Shiki in an attempt to convince Akemi. He had not, however, anticipated her answer.

'Oh, but I have a pretty good eye for people. You, for example, used to be a hooligan, didn't you? Yes? I'll bet you went completely off the rails when you were a student? Didn't you? Hmm?'

Unfortunate for Shiki, she was completely correct.

13

Ryūhei Tomura was the police detectives' sole target. That remained an unchangeable fact, whether they were dealing with one dead body or two, or whether it was morning or afternoon.

But there had been one major development: it was more or less confirmed that Ryūhei Tomura had found an accomplice in Morio Ukai. When they visited him at his office that morning, the detective had pretended he knew nothing about the case, but in fact he was secretly involved. Sunagawa and Shiki were both fuming at the realisation. But it did make locating Ryūhei Tomura easier.

The detectives decided to go with the ultimate weapon in their arsenal: the stake-out. Not of Ryūhei's residence, but the Morio Ukai Detective Agency.

'I wonder whether they'll actually return here.' Shiki wasn't quite convinced. His boss, however , seemed quite sure.

'They will definitely return. Just think about it. Unlike Ryūhei Tomura, Morio Ukai isn't likely to suspect that the police are after him as well. He didn't incriminate himself when we visited his office this morning, he used a fake name when he impersonated a police detective, and he was also wearing a disguise. How can he have guessed that we've seen through his disguise? Therefore, he still thinks he's safe. So it's only natural that he would return to his office. This time we'll catch them.'

The two police detectives were sitting in their parked car. The multi-tenant building where the detective agency was located hardly had any visitors during the day. It was a rather lonely building. The number of visitors started to grow slightly from dusk on, because of the bars in the building opening for business.

Several hours had passed since sunset, and it had become dark. At eight o'clock, an imported car passed by theirs and stopped in the parking lot.

'Boss, it's a Renault! It's Morio Ukai!'

A man stepped out of the car. It was indeed Morio Ukai. Once they knew it was their man, the two detectives jumped out of the police car. Ukai, walking from the parking lot to the front entrance of the building, was hemmed in and unable to move.

He was not taken aback, however, and greeted them jovially.

'Well, well, it's the gentlemen from the police. Good evening.'

'Go—good evening.'

Ukai's genial attitude prompted Sunagawa to return the greeting. Sunagawa is at the core always a polite man. 'Err, no, forget about formalities. We have business with you.'

'What kind of business?'

'Don't be funny. You know who we're talking about. Ryūhei Tomura.'

'Oh, you still haven't found him? Hmm, I never imagined him to be the persevering type.'

'Still playing the fool? We know you're hiding him. So tell us where he is.'

'I don't know anything. I already told you this morning.'

'So you did. But tell me then, why did you visit White Wave Apartments this afternoon accompanied by Tomura?Hm?'

'That wasn't me. Probably just someone who looks like me.'

118

'No, it was you,' Sunagawa persisted. 'We saw you ourselves, so there's no mistake.'

'You saw me? And where did this happen?'

'Near Saiwaichō Park. You and a young man, who was nearly run over when he stepped out of your car, remember? Your young companion was Ryūhei Tomura.'

'Ho—how!' Even Ukai couldn't conceal his shock.

'You see, it was Shiki here who nearly drove over him. I was sitting next to him. So you and Tomura were there, right in front of us. He was wearing a plain suit, exactly the same as the one you're wearing now. He was also wearing a baseball cap and sunglasses. And you were driving that Renault there in the parking lot. What's more, two men dressed exactly like you visited White Wave Apartments, pretending to be police detectives and questioning Akemi Ninomiya, who was there. Care to explain?'

'No, but....'

'We could give you a flat cap and a pair of glasses and ask Akemi Ninomiya to identify you.'

Ukai seemed nervous, but he wasn't about to give up easily. 'Hmmm, could I exercise my right to remain silent in this situation?'

'Still trying to keep silent, eh? Then I'll have to ask you to accompany us to the police station.'

'I don't want any trouble.'

'I seem to recall your sign said something else.'

'I was thinking of getting rid of that sign....' Ukai began, but then he changed his mind and decided to obey the police. 'Okay, I'll come with you then, whether it's to the station or to prison or anywhere else. But I warn you, it's a waste of time.'

'Don't worry,' said Sunagawa. 'Time is something we have plenty of.'

That was one of the strengths of the police force.

14

And now it's time for the final important character to make his appearance. It could be said that he plays the most important part in the story. But this is a very unique person. Sex: male. Age: unknown. Address: none. Occupation: none. Simply put, he belongs to the group of people who tend to live in cardboard houses and are commonly referred to as the homeless.

As far as the police who were searching for him were concerned, Ryūhei Tomura was just a simple college student with no connection to the homeless. It was Morio Ukai who had introduced him to them.

Once the police learnt of the murder of Kōsaku Moro in White Wave Apartments, Ukai managed to convince Ryūhei of the dangers of hiding in a conventional spot, and suggested he become one of the homeless.

This happened, of course, several hours before Ukai himself was detained by the police.

Ukai was convinced that a cardboard house beneath the bridge would be the safest hiding place. But was he right? Ryūhei had always thought that the police always kept an eye on the homeless, so he feared that hiding there would be even more dangerous.

But Ukai was adamant about it. 'Don't worry. When the police are looking for places where a college student would hide, they'll check with classmates, family, other relatives, girl or boyfriend, classmates from previous schools. That's where their focus will be. The homeless? That's a blind spot. So you'll be safe there. Nobody in the police force would ever connect a college student and a homeless person in their minds. It's like watermelon and *natto*, or *miso* and ice cream.'

The comparisons were a bit odd, but Ryūhei finally got the point and agreed. Don't be surprised that he managed to be convinced by such flimsy logic. First of all, he had become a suspect in the murder of Yuki Konno and then, with the discovery of the body of Moro by the police, Ryūhei's future was hanging by a thread. A ravelled thread in a storm.

So, you can't blame him for following Ukai's directions.

Ukai brought Ryūhei to the Nishisaiwai Bridge across the Ika River. It was only one of many bridges crossing the river and, just like the others, many homeless could be found living under it.

Ukai led the way to the base of the bridge. The eaves of two cardboard houses were aligned there, even though they don't actually have eaves. Ukai took Ryūhei to one of them.

Ukai referred to the man inside as Kinzō. The name *Kinzō* literally means "moneybags" but Ryūhei had never met a man who so splendidly represented the complete opposite of the meaning of his name.

Ryūhei was surprised to discover that the cardboard house was larger inside than he had expected, and that Kinzō was actually a hygienic person (relatively speaking), but still, this was a sorry living.

The only moneybags found here were the ones you'd dream about in your sleep. Of course, moneybags were just a fantasy for Ryūhei, too.

It was incredibly uncomfortable inside the house. Chairs were too much to wish for, of course, but what really made things awkward was the fact that the walls were made of paper. You couldn't even lean against them, so Ryūhei curled up on the floor.

Ukai, on the other hand, made himself comfortable, as if it were his own home. Ryūhei wondered what the relation between the two men was, so he asked Ukai when Kinzō went outside.

'Kinzō is a trustworthy partner of mine. I occasionally hire him to assist me. He might look scruffy, but he's actually quite sharp. And he knows how to keep silent, so he's the perfect guy to ask to hide someone. At the very least, I can assure you you're safer here than in my office, or in your flat. Hey, Kinzō!'

Ukai called to the man outside. His bearded face peered in.

'Yes, boss?'

'Here's his accommodation fee. Take it,' said Ukai as he passed a few bills to Kinzō. 'Make sure the police don't get him. Although I don't believe they'll ever come here.'

'Leave it up to me. Your guest is my guest, I'll make sure he's safe.'

Kinzō hit his chest with his fist as he turned to Ryūhei.

'So the police are after you? Poor kid.'

Ryūhei felt a slight shock realising the man felt sorry for him. The police might be after him, but the situation was not so dramatic that a person without a home should feel pity for him.

'The police might be after me, but I didn't do anything. We'll probably work something out.'

But was it really that easy to work something out? Even Ryūhei himself wasn't convinced. Why was he running away? When he thought deeply about it, he realised there was no real reason. It had all started when he ran away from a murder scene, just because the deaths of Kōsaku Moro and Yuki Konno, and the locked room, became entangled and bewildered him. He once again regretted the grave mistake he had made.

But he was not brave enough yet to surrender to the police.

'Are you hungry? I have some food here.'

Kinzō was trying to be kind, but Ryūhei was worried about what would be served.

'I'm not feeling hungry,' he replied tersely.

'You don't have to be polite here,' Kinzō insisted.

Ukai chimed in. 'Yes, don't hold back. The food Kinzō brings back is pretty good. It's just a bit creepy that he never tells me where it comes from…'

'…'

This world was hard to keep up with for a normal college student.

'If you're not hungry, how about a drink?' Kinzō changed the subject. 'I found something good. There are some snacks here too, so how about a drink together? I prefer to drink in company. Kid, you look as though you enjoy a drink.'

'A drink?'

What if he was offered something weird? Ryūhei remained vigilant. He'd heard about these people trying methanol in their craving for alcohol. 'Look here, it's a bottle of Kiyomori sake. And you don't have to worry, as it hasn't even been opened yet.'

And indeed, a bottle of Kiyomori appeared right in front of them. Ryūhei was surprised to see the familiar brand again, after what he'd had the day before. But that was not the only surprise awaiting him.

Kinzō proceeded to pull out small crescent-shaped fried rice crackers, potato crisps, salami slices, cheese *tara* (cheese & cod sticks) and pistachios out of the plastic bag he was holding. Some of the snacks had been opened, others were still sealed. Ryūhei had seen all of these last night!

He looked at the words printed on the plastic bag. It said, "Hanaoka Liquors", just as he had expected. Ryūhei twisted his head.

'Haha, what a coincidence,' Ukai started to joke. 'To come across a plastic bag of Hanaoka Liquors here.'

But Ukai and Ryūhei had the same idea in mind. There was only one possible explanation.

When Ryūhei had fled from Moro's flat that morning, he had thrown the Hanaoka Liquors bag, with the sake and snacks inside, into a garbage can in Saiwaichō Park. The bag he had himself thrown away had now appeared right in front of his eyes.

'Kinzō, where did you find the booze and snacks?' asked Ukai.

'I didn't find them anywhere, the guy who moved in next door gave them to me. Like a present for his new neighbour,' replied Kinzō.

The unexpected explanation took Ukai aback for a moment.

'So that neighbour found it. In the park,' Ryūhei suggested.

'Probably. Haha, what a small world!' said Ukai, amused. 'But it means you don't have to worry. You of all people know where this food comes from, so you don't have to be afraid. You can safely eat

122

and drink all this. You can just pick the unopened snacks, if you prefer.'

Ukai opened the bag of pistachio nuts as he spoke and offered some to Ryūhei.

'I guess you're right.'

Ryūhei seemed to feel more at ease now, and took a few handfuls. He also picked up the paper cup into which Kinzō had poured the sake.

'To a curious coincidence!'

'Cheers! But what's this about a coincidence?

Ryūhei had to laugh at Kinzō's puzzled face.

'Boss, are you having a drink too?'

'No, I'm fine. I still have to drive.'

'Eh!' Ryūhei cried out in shock. 'You're leaving?'

'Of course. I'm not the one being sought by the police.'

At that point Ukai didn't imagine that his name had already become a focus of the police investigation.

Ryūhei clutched Ukai's sleeve like a child clinging to his parents. 'Wait! You can't leave me here all alone!'

'Come on, you can't expect me to stay in this dirty, err, I mean small place. The three of us can't all sleep here. I'm returning to my office. I'll need to think about everything that happened today. I might stumble upon a new lead if I can think by myself about the mystery of the locked room and the meaning of the odd expression on Moro's face.'

Ryūhei couldn't think of any reason to protest.

Then Ukai added: 'Oh, and speaking of new leads, I wasn't exaggerating when I told you Kinzō is sharp. Tell him about the mystery of the locked room. He might come up with some original ideas.'

'A locked room?' asked Kinzō, looking puzzled.

'He'll tell you about it. I'm leaving now. Don't catch cold. I'll see you tomorrow morning,' said Ukai as he left.

15

Ukai had not been on his guard at all when he returned to his office, so he had fallen right into the detectives' trap and quickly given up. At the moment he was sitting in the back seat of the patrol car crossing the Nishisaiwai Bridge. Would he spend the night sleeping in a cell, or would they start questioning him right away and not let him sleep? Whatever the case may be, it was obvious Ukai wouldn't have the time to think by himself about the murders. It was also rather unlikely he'd be able to keep his promise to Ryūhei to return in the morning.

Ryūhei, on the other hand, could not have imagined that a police car with Ukai in it was passing over his head at that very moment.

It was about eight-fifteen in the evening.

Kinzō and Ryūhei were already quite intoxicated.

Ryūhei, who had loosened up after a few drinks, suddenly recalled what Ukai had mentioned to him as he left. Ukai had called Kinzō a sharp guy. If Ryūhei told him about the mystery of the locked room, he might come up with some useful suggestions.

Ryūhei was of course doubtful about that. A homeless person who turns out to be a great detective sounded like a modern-day fable, not realistic at all. Especially if the detective was supposed to be the scruffy middle-aged man in front of him.

But despite these impressions, he decided to confide the details of the case to Kinzō. One reason was that, at this point, Ryūhei was ready to grasp at any straw. (Not that Kinzō was like straw.) Another reason was that an evening without television or stereo felt insufferably long to Ryūhei, and he was getting bored.

Ryūhei explained the major points of the case. He especially focused on the fact that the locked room was sealed in two ways: by the door chain and by the presence of the woman (Akemi Ninomiya) near the crime scene. How had the murderer escaped? How had he gone unnoticed by Akemi? Wasn't that impossible?

When he was done with his story, Ryūhei looked at Kinzō expectantly. It wasn't as if Ryūhei himself knew what had happened, but as he related the events to Kinzō, he subconsciously came to feel like the quizmaster in a television show.

Kinzō had been sitting cross-legged as he listened to Ryūhei. When the quizmaster was done, he tapped his knee a few times.

'Ha, that's nothing. That locked room mystery couldn't be simpler! Easy peasy!'

'Easy peasy?'

Living apart from society must have affected the fellow's linguistic senses.

'Have you really worked it out? I have to warn you, the "internal bleeding inside a locked room" theory is out. Mr. Ukai went for that, but had to give up on that idea.'

'Hehe, I have something else.'

There was a triumphant grin on Kinzō's face. Judging by his reaction, he knew exactly what the "internal bleeding inside a locked room" theory was. Perhaps he wasn't just any homeless guy.

'To summarise your story, the door chain of Flat 4 of White Wave Apartments was locked, and the windows were locked with crescent locks. So, nobody could have gone in or out.'

'Yes.That's it.'

'And the testimony of that Akemi girl who was working on her motorbike near the gate also confirms that nobody got in or out.'

'Yes, that's why it's a locked room murder.'

'How curious.'

'Exactly! So how did the murderer escape?'

Kinzō shook his head as he rubbed his unshaven chin.

'No, I meant that it's curious how smart people like you and the boss didn't think of it earlier yourselves.'

'Think of what?'

'The murderer was never at the scene,' said Kinzō, as he gulped down the remaining contents of his paper cup in one go. 'What else could the explanation be? If nobody could have gone in or out, then the answer is that the killer never set foot inside. If you simply think about it, it becomes as clear as day.'

'I suppose that's a thought, but it doesn't explain a thing. Because Moro was actually stabbed with a knife. So there had to be someone there to kill him.'

'Of course there was. But just because the victim was in the bathroom, doesn't mean the murderer had to be there too. The murderer was outside the bathroom.'

'Outside?'

For a moment Ryūhei thought Kinzō meant the dressing room or the hallway, but it didn't seem as though he was talking about those places. Ryūhei eagerly waited to hear what Kinzō would say next.

'The killer was outside the bathroom when they stabbed the victim , who was inside the bathroom.'

'Eh! From outside the bathroom!? By outside, you mean outside the flat?'

'Yes. There's a window that opens to the outside in that bathroom, I believe?'

'Yes, but it's not a window you can open completely. It tilts open, and even when it's completely open no one can pass through it.'

'But kid, no person needs to pass through that window. It's enough that a knife can pass through it. Perhaps the weapon was more like a spear than a knife.'

'A spear! Aha, I get what you're trying to say now!'

'You're slow, kid. I thought of it the moment I heard you tell me the story.' Kinzō's superior attitude was partially due to the amount of drink he'd consumed. 'The killer made a kind of spear by attaching the knife to a rod. They used that weapon to stab their victim from the other side of the bathroom window. So the bathroom window didn't need to be wide open. The fact the door and windows were locked from the inside? Irrelevant. The killer managed to stab the victim in his side with the weapon, and it's obvious what happened next.'

'The killer detached the knife from the rod and threw it inside the bathroom through the window.'

'Exactly. And that's how a locked room mystery was created. Couldn't be simpler!'

Kinzō clapped his hands as if to indicate the case was closed and started drinking from his paper cup again.

'But would it really go as smoothly as that? Wouldn't it be pretty easy to miss your target with a spear?'

Kinzō appeared to have expected this question. 'Not a problem. Even if the killer missed their target, it would not have been a crucial mistake. How would the target ever recognise an assailant who stabbed him with a spear through a small gap? The target wouldn't even be able to chase after them. The only thing the killer had to do if they missed was to run away. Very likely they'd get away, too. Am I right? Heheh, what a crafty plan.'

'That's true enough.'

Ryūhei had to admit it was a very clever line of reasoning. At the very least, it made more sense in a lot of ways than Ukai's hypothesis.

But there was still one major flaw in Kinzō's theory. The spear trick would only work if they could overcome it. But Ryūhei chose not to raise the objection with Kinzō yet. He wanted to give it some thought himself first.

'Well, I'm really impressed by your deductive talents, Mr. Kinzō! You managed to solve the mystery of the locked room just by listening to my story. You've been a great help. Let's tell Mr. Ukai first thing in the morning about what you just told me. With a bit of luck, it will all be cleared up.'

Ryūhei heaped praise on Kinzō in order to end the talk.

126

'Happy to hear I could be of help. Now have some more drink, kid. And have some snacks, too. They were given to me, so don't be shy.'

'Thanks.'

Ryūhei experienced a sense of *déjà vu* as he put his hand in the bag of nuts.

Last night, he had also spent the evening with drinks and snacks. Together with Kōsaku Moro. He was not here anymore. Yet Ryūhei was repeating the previous evening, drinking and eating nuts. It was a weird sensation. But that wasn't all. There was something else....

In his intoxicated mind, out-of-focus images of last night and this evening started to overlap. By tomorrow, maybe the image would finally come into focus.

For now, Ryūhei's long, long day of tightrope walking was finally at an end.

CHAPTER FOUR: THE THIRD DAY

1

The first thing that manifested itself before Ryūhei's eyes the following morning was a dirty brown plank.

It took a while before he could recall what the thing was doing in his line of sight. When he finally shook off his drowsiness, he recalled that he had spent the night in a cardboard house.

He finally realised he wasn't looking at a plank: it was the roof of his new home. He hadn't noticed it last night, but the roof was rather low. Staring at it too long would lead to a fearful, oppressive feeling. In some ways, the cardboard house was somewhat similar to, yet also completely different from, the free, open life in a camping tent.

Ryūhei raised his body in the cramped space. The master of this mansion, Kinzō, was lying near his feet. He was still sleeping. Perhaps he was enjoying some delicious food in his dreams. So why pull him cruelly back to the realm of reality? Ryūhei got up silently.

He could almost hear his stiff body creak. He recalled that he had woken up like this yesterday as well. He had been lying on the plank flooring of the dressing room then. Today he woke up on cardboard laid out on the ground. Given how stiff his body felt today, he reckoned that lying on plank flooring had been the better option.

But perhaps today was still the better option, as this time he wasn't confronted with a dead body.

But wait!

Ryūhei carefully poked the homeless person lying near his feet with his finger. Kinzō reacted to the stimulus in his side by twisting his body. Phew, he was not dead.

Then again, nobody is likely to wake up next to a dead body two days in a row.

No major problems yet this morning then, but Ryūhei's worries were about the future. What about tomorrow morning? Perhaps he'd be waking up on the concrete floor of a prison cell: a very possible scenario, given his current situation.

Ryūhei stepped outside. He checked his watch. It was past eight-thirty. He walked over to the Ika River to wash his face, but one look told him the water was not clean, so he changed his mind.

129

He was hungry, but he wasn't in the mood for breakfast in the morning sun on the riverside. Ryūhei sat down in the long grass, partially to hide himself. He put his mind to the matter he had stopped thinking about last night.

Ryūhei had been highly impressed by the reasoning laid out so fluently by Kinzō the previous night. The killer might indeed have used a spear as the murder weapon. However, it was not a perfect theory. There was one major flaw.

Suppose the killer had indeed succeeded in stabbing Moro through the bathroom window. They would have been in full sight of Akemi, who had been working on her motorcycle near the front gate.

Kinzō had probably arrived at his theory because Ryūhei had not explained in detail where the bathroom window was located. It was actually situated right next to the front door. So Akemi, who had a good view of the front door of Flat 4 from where she was standing, would automatically also have a good view of the bathroom window. She would have noticed any suspicious figure standing there. Especially if, as Kinzō had reasoned, the figure was holding a spear.

That was the ultimate obstacle. The only person to appear in Akemi's testimony was Kōsaku Moro, who had gone to and returned from Hanaoka Liquors. There was not a hint of any other person in her story. That is why Ukai's theory had to be abandoned, and it was clear that, for the same reason, Kinzō's "spear entering the locked room" theory would also need to be discarded.

But Ryūhei couldn't stop thinking about the two "internal bleeding inside the locked room" and "spear entering the locked room" theories.

Both theories had been discredited by Akemi Ninomiya's testimony, which had been crucial. But you could also look at it another way: the only thing standing in the way of either locked room theory was her testimony.

And therefore the trustworthiness of her testimony became a matter of considerable importance.

Up until now, Ryūhei and Ukai had considered Akemi Ninomiya as an objective third party. But the mystery would never be solved if they simply took her word for it.

Wasn't it therefore also necessary to harbour doubts about her testimony?

Either solution to the locked room mystery would be viable if Akemi Ninomiya's testimony were to be discredited. So, didn't it make more sense to doubt it, rather than be forced to produce yet another theory?

Perhaps Akemi Ninomiya had been lying to them.

But why? He couldn't come up with a clear reason. But he did think of at least two possibilities. The first was that the murderer was someone close to Akemi, and that she had lied to protect them. And the second was that Akemi herself was the murderess.

Surprisingly enough, they were not possibilities that Ryūhei could rule out right away.

The longer he thought about the case, the more he felt he couldn't just sit there doing nothing. He reasoned that it was first necessary to tell Ukai about Kinzō's theory. After that, they could discuss what to do next.

Ryūhei got up and walked back to the cardboard house. Kinzō was still fast asleep. He had apparently fallen into an even deeper slumber, because now he was snoring. Ryūhei didn't feel like waking him up, so he closed the door (a plywood plank) again. He left the premises, hoping that one day he could repay the meal and roof he had been offered. He climbed up the river bank, walked along the main road, and hailed a taxi to the Morio Ukai Detective Agency.

Normally the trip would only have taken five minutes, but Ryūhei finally arrived at his destination twenty-five minutes later, having got stuck in the morning rush hour. But, because Ryūhei could not very well just walk out in the open, he'd had no other choice but to sit and wait to see when he'd arrive.

Just as the day before, Ryūhei went up the emergency stairs in the rear of the multi-tenant building, opened the heavy door there, and slipped inside. The sensation of feeling out of breath and dizzy was also exactly the same as the day before. The sight of the silent, gloomy hallway of the second floor made Ryūhei feel as if he were watching a replay of the previous day. He quickly made his way to the Morio Ukai Detective Agency sign and rang the bell. There was no answer, but Ryūhei simply assumed Ukai was still asleep.

He placed his hand on the knob and tried turning it. It turned without any problem. He had expected the door chain to be locked, but to his surprise, the door was completely unlocked.

At this point, Ryūhei should have begun to be alarmed, but he merely thought Ukai should be more careful when locking up.

'Good grief, he's a detective, but he doesn't lock his door when he goes to sleep? What if I were an assassin?'

In reality, private detectives aren't likely to be targeted by assassins. At least, probably not.

It was cool inside. But even that didn't make Ryūhei realise the detective was absent. He was pretty slow-witted for a person on the run. Ryūhei walked past the couch and desk that doubled as a reception space, and went to the private quarters beyond. It was where the half-broken couch which Ukai used as his bed was located. Ryūhei did find the couch in the room, but not the detective.

It was only then that Ryūhei started to feel anxious. Ukai wasn't there. It was cold inside. The front door was unlocked. And he was inside, all alone.

By the time Ryūhei realised he was the mouse in the trap, it was already too late.

He turned around to find two suspicious men standing there. Just to be clear, there was nothing inherently suspicious about them, he just thought they looked dubious. Ryūhei, who remained surprisingly calm, was taller than the two men, and so looked down at them .

'Who are you?'

The calm manner in which he asked the question made the two men nervous. The younger fished for something in his inner coat pocket and produced the familiar black leather notebook, which he showed to Ryūhei.

'My ID. You are Ryūhei Tomura, I assume?'

Ryūhei looked carefully at the notebook.

'…'

It was a real one. It didn't say "Lucky Notebook".

'Hey, hey!' The young police detective thought it was bizarre how intensely Ryūhei was staring at the notebook. 'You don't need to stare so hard at it. We aren't fake detectives using fake IDs, like you.'

'Ah, aha.'

Ryūhei suddenly felt completely drained. His life on the run had started the previous morning, and realising it was now over after one whole day gave him a sense of relief. He felt as though he'd been on the run for over a week already. Enough was enough. Ryūhei didn't have the spirit to resist anymore.

It was the middle-aged police detective's turn to speak: 'Morio Ukai has been our guest since last night. We'll have to ask you to come down to the station as well. Two people in your circle of acquaintances have died under curious circumstances, one after the other. We think you might have some explaining to do. You have your rights, of course, but how about some cooperation with the investigation? We're busy too, so we don't have the time to play hide-and-seek with you.'

132

His tone indicated he was fed up with all the nonsense.

Ryūhei was being questioned by the two police detectives in one of the interrogation rooms at the station. The older detective introduced himself as Chief Inspector Sunagawa, the younger one as Shiki. Ryūhei memorised their names.

He answered all their questions and related all that had happened up until then, from how he was confronted with the mystery of the locked room, about Morio Ukai's "internal bleeding inside the locked room" theory, about Kinzō's "spear entering the locked room" theory and even his own "the murderess is Akemi Ninomiya" theory.

Needless to say, the two detectives had been been unprepared for this. When Ryūhei gave up without any resistance, they had expected that he would simply confess to the crimes and that the case would be over and done with. But even Ryūhei noticed how the expression on the faces of the detectives changed the more he talked. Which was only natural: they had expected a confession, but instead they were presented with the mysterious matter of the locked room. Whilst Ryūhei didn't know whether they believed him or not, he was glad they were listening to him seriously.

It took quite some time for him to finish his story. He shot an inquisitive look at the detectives. Shiki immediately declared he didn't believe a word of it, but Chief Inspector Sunagawa said quietly: 'Sorry, but I'll have to ask you to go over it again from the start.'

Ryūhei was ready to tell the story as often as necessary if it would convince the police.

2

Finally. It has taken quite some time. On the third day after the first murder occurred, the separate plotlines of the hunting and hunted duos can now converge into a single storyline. The quick-witted reader will probably have guessed that this story that tends to repeat itself will soon come to an end. Of course, even readers who are not that quick could probably tell that, considering the number of pages remaining, it wasn't likely that more dead bodies would turn up.

All the factors necessary to solve the case have now come together. The police detectives who had expected that the case would be solved with Ryūhei's confession had been surprised at first, but the problem of the locked room mystery suddenly presented to them did manage to capture their attention.

That even the unenthusiastic Chief Inspector Sunagawa suddenly had a gleam in his eye now, was of course a fact worth mentioning. At the beginning it was said that the Ikagawa City Police Station would not be itself without his presence, and that was no exaggeration. He apparently realised he was in possession of some important clues.

So let's have Chief Inspector Sunagawa himself explain the whole case… wait, that is what I'd like to do, but before that, we need to set the stage.

So let's return to our roots, and have Sunagawa sit by the canal again. The time: three o'clock in the afternoon. The interrogation of Ryūhei Tomura had been paused for a moment. The weather: clear skies. Gentle wind. There are perhaps two or three jellyfish floating in the water.

Chief Inspector was using a beer case as a chair at the canal's edge. To an outsider, he might have looked like the quintessential elderly police detective who was simply killing time and waiting for his retirement, but they couldn't have been more wrong. Chief Inspector Sunagawa was scribbling furiously in his notebook. Not his police notebook, but his own notebook used for memos. He would think and write, write and think. Whenever he wasn't pleased with something, he would rip the page out. The process repeated itself.

'Chief Inspector!' It was, of course, Shiki who was approaching him. 'What are you doing here counting jellyfish? Let's get back to the interrogation.…'

'Bah!' snorted Sunagawa. 'Who's counting jellyfish at such a crucial time?'

'Weren't you counting them?'

'I already finished counting them. Don't worry, the sky will stay clear.'

'I wasn't thinking of the weather, I was thinking of the investigation.'

'So was I. I've been giving it a great deal of thought,' said Sunagawa as he put the notebook back in his coat pocket. 'Shiki, what's your impression of Tomura's story? He woke up next to a body in the bathroom, the door chain was locked, the windows were locked, and he was the only one inside. But he claims he wasn't the murderer. Do you believe this locked room mystery story of his?'

'Of course not, who would? He's the murderer. He was the only person with Kōsaku Moro on the night of the murder. He was probably also the one who killed Yuki Konno. For one thing, if he was innocent, why was he running away from us?'

'He said the locked room situation made him lose his head, and that he didn't think the police would believe him. That's not entirely unreasonable.'

'Really? The locked room has to be a pure invention.'

'But don't you think it's a bit too bizarre for a made-up story? A murderer will lie to protect himself. But the locked room situation he describes eliminates everyone as the killer except for himself. His testimony only makes things worse for him. That doesn't make any sense.'

'Perhaps he's just stupid.'

'Perhaps he's just too simple-minded.'

Shiki's eyes opened wide in utter disbelief. 'Chief Inspector, do you really believe his story? The murders of Yuki Konno and Kōsaku Moro occurred within a very short time-frame. And, in terms of distance, it was just a one-minute walk. The medical examiner said they were both probably killed by the same weapon. There is no way these two cases occurred completely independently of each other. And if they are indeed connected, then you arrive automatically at Ryūhei Tomura. That's the only possible interpretation, surely?'

'Hmm, perhaps.'

Whilst he did not deny the possibility, Chief Inspector Sunagawa's face betrayed that he was still considering the possibility someone other than Ryūhei could have done it.

'Tomura said that Akemi Ninomiya was a suspect. What do you think?'

'Hahaha, you mean that fantastical method of using a knife as a spear? You must be kidding.'

'But it is possible to stab someone from the other side of that bathroom window.'

'But sir, it's not about whether it's possible or not. Even supposing that Akemi Ninomiya is the murderess, how would she know that Kōsaku Moro would take a bath at ten-thirty? This so-called murder method doesn't work unless you can somehow know beforehand the exact time the victim is going to take a shower. Because the weapon needs to be prepared ahead of time. And why would she need to go through that much trouble anyway? You saw it yourself. She's the landlord. She can use her duplicate keys to walk into any room at any time. Why would she resort to using a spear and creating some kind of locked room mystery? By doing that, she'd just make herself look more suspicious. She, the murderess? Unthinkable.'

'You have a point.'

'So Tomura is our killer.'

'I'm still not entirely convinced,' said Sunagawa reluctantly. 'There's something about that story he told us that bothers me. Just a small detail, but I can't get it out of my head. And if I'm right, we might have a rather interesting problem in front of us.'

'Boss, why are you speaking so vaguely? In other words, you don't think Tomura is our guy?'

'Let's say it's possible he's innocent. We're still in a grey area.'

'Really? In my eyes, he couldn't look any guiltier.'

'Okay, let's see who's right then.'

'Is it that easy?' Shiki was taken aback by Sunagawa's relaxed mood. 'Working out whether he's really the killer is not as easy as a game of rock-paper-scissors, sir.'

Sunagawa got up from the beer case. 'Of course not. But I know a way. Shiki, find me a meeting room or visitor's room, I don't care what, as long as it has a television and video player.'

'Is this about *Massacre Manor,* the tape he rented from Astro? What about it?'

'Let's both watch the film together.'

A stunned expression appeared on Shiki's face.

'*Massacre Manor*? Don't you remember the guy from the rental shop said that it was so boring it would be a waste of time?'

'Let's just see how boring it really is.'

Shiki naturally didn't understand what was in his superior's mind, but he did as he was told.

3

The equipment requested by Chief Inspector Sunagawa was quickly set up in the interrogation room. A television and a video player were placed in the corner of a room which had been witness to countless interrogations. It was a unique sight.

'Sorry, sir, I tried to get us a meeting room, but they're being used for the crime prevention lectures. We'll have to make do here.'

Sunagawa sat down on one of the folding chairs as he watched Shiki set things up. 'I don't mind. Actually, this room might even be more fitting. Doesn't it remind you of anything, this space?'

Shiki's hands stopped working on the wiring as he asked for an explanation.

'Feels just like Kōsaku Moro's home theatre here. The room has always been sound-proof, and now we have a television and video player here. It's basically our own home theatre.'

'Aha. So this is like a reconstruction of the night of the crime. But how will this help us solve the case? Oh, I guess you won't tell me anyway.'

'Exactly. Not yet anyway.'

'I knew it. And this should make it work now.'

After checking the wires, Shiki switched the equipment on and pressed the play button. Suddenly the screen was filled by a close-up shot of the private parts of a woman as a low howl echoed through the room. The loudness of the volume and the visuals were so shocking that Sunagawa fell off his chair.

Shiki quickly pressed the stop button. 'Terribly sorry, sir! Guess this is a black-market video. Must've been seized when rolling up an illegal shop.'

'What's it doing in the player?'

Shiki shrugged. 'Lots of officers here work hard and put in a lot of time. So let's pretend we didn't notice. Don't forget that ninety percent of the Ikagawa Police Force is male.'

Shiki's excuse was flimsy, but he removed the tape and placed it beside the television. He inserted the tape of *Massacre Manor* instead. The player was about to start automatically, but Shiki stopped it.

'Sir, we're ready.'

'Okay, let's call Ryūhei Tomura in then.'

'Right,' said Shiki. He was about to leave the room when he turned around. 'What about that detective?'

'Well, okay then, he can come as well,' the boss agreed grudgingly.

Ryūhei Tomura and "that detective" Morio Ukai were let into the interrogation room one after another. When Ryūhei saw Ukai, he hugged him emotionally, even though it was only one day since they had last seen each other. At first the two were happy to have been reunited, but their talk soon became less touching.

'Why did you get caught!? I was going to keep silent about you!' grumbled Ukai. And indeed, he had not revealed Ryūhei's whereabouts to Shiki and Sunagawa despite their threats.

Betrayal had not been on Ukai's mind at all. While he was enjoying their "hospitality" he kept pestering them with requests for rice bowls with fried pork cutlets and sushi, and the two policemen were getting quite annoyed with him. This was the detective's method of covering his client's back, even when in captivity.

But Ryūhei Tomura had allowed himself to get caught, so Ukai's efforts had been for naught. He was quite irritated.

Ryūhei talked fast as he tried to explain what had happened.

'This morning I went to your office, and they were there waiting for me. I thought you'd be there.'

'That was stupid. You should have called first to see if I was there.'

'Yes, that was foolish perhaps,' admitted Ryūhei meekly, but then launched a counterattack. 'But didn't you get caught first?'

The detective couldn't quite find the right words. 'Ahem. You see...'

He didn't want to confess his imported car had given him away. It was too embarrassing. Chief Inspector Sunagawa was grinning as he looked at the two fighting.

'But why have we been brought here, anyway?'

'Eh? I don't know.' Ryūhei shook his head.

Sunagawa stepped forward as if to answer their questions.

'There's something I want the two of you to see. Just to tie up some loose ends. You know it, *Massacre Manor*. Err, a 1977 film by director Ryūtarō Kawauchi, from Kantō Film Corporation. Runtime: Two hours and thirty minutes,' Sunagawa read from the label on the tape. 'Mr. Tomura, is this the same film you claim you watched with Kōsaku Moro?'

'Claim? Claim?!' Ryūhei cried, red in the face. 'Yes, that's the one. I watched it with Mr. Moro on the night of the twenty-eighth of February! I also remember the time exactly. We started at seven-thirty in the evening and finished it at ten on the dot.'

And that was why he had nothing at all to do with the murder of Yuki Konno at nine forty-two that evening. That was the story Ryūhei stuck to throughout his interrogation. But when Shiki or Sunagawa asked him for proof of that, he always stumbled and fell silent.

Sunagawa didn't feel like repeating that same conversation all over again. He offered the men a seat.

'Sit down and let's watch a film together. Look around, don't you think this room looks like that home theatre back at White Wave Apartments? And we're going to screen the same film too. Just watch it the same way you did on the twenty-eighth.'

Ryūhei and Ukai both had doubtful looks on their faces as they sat down on their chairs.

'Okay, Shiki, roll the film,' said Sunagawa as he checked his wristwatch. 'It's exactly four o'clock now. The film is two hours and thirty minutes long, so we'll be done by six-thirty. Let's enjoy the film.'

Shiki pushed the play button and started the tape. The logo of Kantō Film Corporation appeared on the screen and the dark, depressing tale of massacre started.

Ten minutes went by, then twenty minutes, then thirty.

The gloomy interrogation room was filled with the visuals and audio filmed a quarter century ago. The memory of intense boredom when he and his friends had watched this film came back to Shiki. It was impossible to count the number of characters on the fingers of two hands, and the relationships between them were strange and convoluted. The story was thus unbelievably slow and the dialogue needlessly lengthy. Another ten minutes of this and Shiki was sure Morpheus was going to knock him out. He was still on duty, so that worried him.

Why go to all this trouble? What was on the Chief Inspector's mind?

Shiki couldn't help but be puzzled by his chief's actions.

Twenty more minutes passed.

Shiki was on the brink of sleep. He looked at Ryūhei, who was sitting next to him. But to his great surprise he saw that Ryūhei was staring vacantly at the screen, his mouth wide open in utter disbelief.

Why would he look like that? Was he so bored? It was the second time he had seen it, and the first was only two days earlier, so why did he appear so surprised by the film now?

'Sto—stop it!'

Suddenly, a cry rang out in the interrogation room. It had come from Ryūhei. Shiki used the remote control to pause the film. He was ready to hear Ryūhei confess that very moment, but Sunagawa seemed still quite relaxed and asked Ryūhei: 'What's the matter? We're only halfway through the film.'

'Yes, I, I get that. But…'

Ryūhei was at a loss for words. But then he looked up and pointed his right index finger at the paused image on the television screen. In a hoarse voice, he cried out: '… But I don't get that! What's this you're showing us!?'

'You shouldn't ask me, this is the film you picked. Ryūtarō Kawauchi's *Massacre Manor*. This is the correct tape, isn't it, Shiki?'

Shiki hadn't quite expected to be addressed and quickly nodded in response to the question.

'Yes, this is definitely *Massacre Manor*... Most certainly.'

'No way....'

Ryūhei was visibly baffled as his whole body trembled vehemently. He turned to the private detective next to him as if to plead for help.

'Is this *Massacre Manor*? Is this the real *Massacre Manor*?'

The private detective was also puzzled by Ryūhei's reaction. His eyes blinked rapidly as he peered into Ryūhei's face.

'Of course this is *Massacre Manor*. What else would it be? Wait, you're not going to tell me that the film you watched with Kōsaku Moro that night wasn't *Massacre Manor* after all?'

'No!' Ryūhei shook his head strongly. 'I mean, I did see *Massacre Manor* with him that night.'

'So what's the matter then?' asked Ukai in confusion.

'But this wasn't the film I saw!' exclaimed Ryūhei. 'The *Massacre Manor* I saw was much more entertaining!!'

4

The interrogation was suspended in silence for a moment. It appeared that only Chief Inspector Sunagawa understood the meaning of the words Ryūhei had just blurted out. Shiki and Ukai were speechless, unable to quite grasp the meaning of what had happened. But the person who was the most confused of them all was Ryūhei himself. Why was his impression of the same film completely different this time? He had never experienced anything like this before.

The paused image on the screen radiated eerily in the silent room.

After a moment of silence, Shiki started to laugh.

'Ha-ha, that's—that's a good one. You're telling me there's a boring *Massacre Manor* and a fun one?'

That was of course impossible.

Ukai thought for a moment before he reacted.

'Perhaps you saw a remake.'

As a student of film, Ryūhei of course knew what Ukai meant.

Some films, especially the hits and masterpieces, are often remade as new films. Sometimes very often, even. For example, *Rickshaw Man* and *The Burmese Harp* both have been filmed twice by Hiroshi Inagaki and Kon Ichikawa respectively. In those cases, the directors of both the original and the remake versions were the same, so much remained familiar, but if a film is remade by a different director, the end result can be very different from the original, even if the title and story remain the same.

But that wasn't the case here.

Shiki answered for Ryūhei.

'That's impossible. There's no way there are two *Massacre Manor* titles, both released in 1977 by Kantō Film Corporation. If the film he claims he saw with Moro two nights ago was *Massacre Manor*, it has to be the exact same film as the one we're watching now.'

Ryūhei nodded.

'Yes, it is the same film. But it's different. But, oh, I can't believe it. It has to be the editing. It's edited completely differently.'

'Editing?' Shiki repeated the word puzzled.

Ryūhei didn't say any more. He was frozen in his chair, cradling his head. Shiki and Ukai seemed completely baffled by his words, so he looked at Sunagawa.

The Chief Inspector explained what was going on.

'A film lover once told me a story. It's supposed to be true, but he might have exaggerated just a little. Anyway, it was a very interesting story, so I remembered it. It's a story about a particular film.

'A particular film had been made. The reception it received was mixed... you might even say negative. But it had been a major project. The amount of resources the studio had poured into the film was no laughing matter. The producers had wanted to submit it to a foreign film festival, but it would never be accepted the way it was. The film was just too long.

'The length didn't matter for a theatrical release in Japan, but to attract the attention of the busy people in the film industry abroad and convince them to devote precious time to view their film, it was best to have a shorter version. So whilst the director had poured his heart and soul into the enterprise, he had no choice but to swallow his pride and start cutting the film. The non-essential scenes had to go. To the creative minds behind the film, that was like cutting themselves up.

'But when the Japanese critics saw the international re-edited version of the film, they all thought to themselves: this version is far better and more entertaining than the long and boring original version. Of course, they didn't say that too loudly in front of the director, who had felt miserable that he'd had to make the cuts.'

Nobody dared interrupt Sunagawa's story. He continued:

'A memorable story, don't you think? Can you believe that the reception of a film can change that much just by cutting it? It's ironic that cutting a film can actually make it better.

'Mr. Tomura, the part in your testimony where you told us about your impressions of *Massacre Manor* has always bothered me. You told us that it was very entertaining, that the film had good pacing with many murders. That puzzled me. You see, I remembered seeing it when I was much younger. But my impression of the film couldn't have been more different than yours.

'Of course, that happens. Everyone can have different opinions about the same film. But that employee from the rental shop—yes, you know, Kazuki Kuwata—was of the same opinion. And Shiki here had also seen the film with his college friends and nobody had liked it. So a lot of people shared my opinion. Basically, *Massacre Manor* is simply too long-winded. But while everyone else thinks *Massacre Manor* is too long, you alone said you liked it.

'Was it simply because your taste in films is different from ours? Possibly. But perhaps, you saw a *different* film from the one we saw. Perhaps the film you saw wasn't the original one, but an *edited* version of *Massacre Manor*. That was what I wanted to know, so that's why I decided we should watch the film together.'

'So that's it...' Ryūhei stammered. 'The *Massacre Manor* I saw with Moro the evening before yesterday had been edited. It had been cut down to a shorter version.'

'Yes. The film we were watching here in this room is the original. The version you were shown was probably thirty minutes shorter.'

Chief Inspector Sunagawa stopped the paused video completely. He took the tape from the player and showed it to Tomura. Shiki had a question for his boss.

'But if someone just decided to cut thirty minutes from a film, wouldn't that mess up the flow of the story and ruin it?'

'Perhaps. Let's ask an expert on that. Mr. Tomura, can you cut a two-and-a-half hour film by thirty minutes without it interrupting the flow of the story?'

Ryūhei's answer was clear.

'That probably wouldn't cause any problems. Thirty minutes isn't much, actually. That's about the amount of time they cut whenever a film is shown on television, in order to fit the time-slot. That's how a two-hour film will actually only run for ninety minutes, without the commercials. Anyone used to the job will be able to cut down thirty minutes. But....'

Ryūhei's explanation then turned into a question.

'But I'm sure this is the tape I got from Kazuki Kuwata at the rental shop. So how did it get edited? Who did that?'

Sunagawa chose his words carefully.

'Yes, that's the crucial question. There are only two possible candidates, if we don't count you. And Kazuki Kuwata is out as well, because he couldn't have known beforehand that you'd come and rent *Massacre Manor* two days ago. And if he didn't know beforehand, he couldn't very well have edited the film and prepared the tape for you. That means there's only one person who could have done it: The person who knew beforehand that you'd be renting *Massacre Manor* on the twenty-eighth of February. And, as you pointed out, a person who would be very familiar with video editing.'

'…'

The outline of the culprit was forming in Ryūhei's mind. It was not easy to accept, but it was the undeniable truth. But that didn't make it less hard to believe.

It was Chief Inspector Sunagawa's voice that broke the silence in the room.

'It was Kōsaku Moro.'

'No!' Ryūhei exclaimed. But in his heart, he knew it to be true.

'It is the truth. He was the one who operated the video equipment that evening, so he could easily have switched the tape you brought with his own shorter version. He is the only one who could have done that. And he could have easily created his own edited version using the equipment at the film company where he works. And he has experience with film editing.'

Ryūhei couldn't deny any of that. No, at this point he had already become convinced it had been Moro. Moro had the talent for it. There was no doubt that if Moro had cut out the non-essential scenes from the long, boring version of *Massacre Manor*, the new short version would be more entertaining than the original. And that's what Ryūhei had been shown.

'But why? Why would he go to all that trouble, just for a prank?'

'He needed to fool the clock. By showing you the short version of the film, he messed up your sense of time. That was his goal. But not just for some prank. It was a deliberate trick by Kōsaku Moro to fake his alibi. Mr. Tomura, you were fooled completely by the trickery.'

'Fake his alibi? Alibi for what?'

Sunagawa finally unveiled the deepest secret of the case.

'Why, an alibi for the murder of Yuki Konno of course. *Yes, it was Kōsaku Moro who murdered her....*'

5

Ryūhei was absolutely dumbfounded, so Sunagawa explained in detail.

'You might not believe it, but it's the truth. I'm absolutely convinced of it. But it's only natural you can't believe it right away. For how could Kōsaku Moro, with whom you watched a film together until ten o'clock two nights ago, have killed Yuki Konno at nine forty-two that same evening? If you just take things at face value, it seems utterly impossible. But it is possible, by preparing that short version of *Massacre Manor*. Let me explain this in order.

'A week ago, you and Moro agreed you were going to watch *Massacre Manor* together on the evening of the twenty-eighth of February in Moro's home theatre. Moro used the week he had to create a shorter version. It wouldn't have been too difficult, given his experience and the equipment at his workplace. That was stage one.

'Now we jump forward to seven o'clock on the evening of the twenty-eighth. You arrived at Moro's flat with the real tape of *Massacre Manor* you'd just rented. At first, you talked a little about work and then Moro offered you something very important. Do you remember what it was?'

'Very important? No, what was it?' Ryūhei asked, cocking his head.

'His bathroom. That was a vital step in his criminal scheme. Kōsaku Moro casually, but determinedly, offered you his bathroom. You didn't suspect a thing, and took a bath. When you were done, Moro offered you a sweat suit, which you put on. At this point, the second stage in Moro's plan was complete. Do you see how? It wasn't the bath itself. It was making you take off your wristwatch because you were having a bath. That was the crucial point of his plan. Mr. Tomura, when you got out of the bath and changed into something more relaxed, I assume you didn't put your wristwatch back on?'

'Oh, now you mention it, I remember. I put my wristwatch, together with my jeans and shirt, in the laundry basket.'

'Yes, that was the natural thing to do. So you got out of bath, and what's the first thing you saw? The television. The seven o'clock news was about to end. It wasn't a coincidence that you saw the news. It was a calculated part of Moro's plan. The end of the seven o'clock news meant it was almost seven-thirty. And that time would be more trustworthy than any clock you would see. Unlike a clock, nobody can just change the time of a television program. That is how that moment, a few minutes before seven-thirty, was planted in your memory.

'That was the third stage of the plan.

'You and Moro then moved to the home theatre. You didn't have to look at any clocks to know it was now around seven-thirty. You gave the real tape of *Massacre Manor* to Moro. He was the one who would put it into the video player and start the film. However, what Moro actually did was to hide the tape he got from you amongst the other tapes on the shelves, and put the tape with the shorter version of *Massacre Manor* into the deck. Do you follow me? Pay attention, it's going to become a bit more difficult from this point on. The runtime of the original *Massacre Manor* is two hours and thirty minutes, just as the label on the tape says. If my calculations are correct however, the shorter version only runs for two hours. It's that difference of thirty minutes that creates Moro's fake alibi. Anyway, Moro had no difficulty swapping the tapes. He also changed the internal timer of the video player by thirty minutes, to show eight o'clock, before he started playing the tape. That was all part of his plan to make two hours appear like two and a half hours to you. A phone call on your mobile would have given away the time difference with the outside world, so naturally he didn't allow you to use one. He didn't forget to be very strict with you about the use of mobile phones. You didn't suspect a thing, and truly believed that the screening of the film started at seven-thirty in the evening and ended at ten o'clock. That was stage four.

'The film ended. Moro himself operated the video deck and removed the tape. It was the tape with the edited version, so he couldn't afford to let you see it. He hid it amongst the countless tapes on the shelves, and retrieved the real tape he had hidden earlier and placed it on top of the player. At that moment you believed it was ten o'clock. You weren't wearing your wristwatch so, led on by Moro, you checked the clock on the video deck, which indicated ten o'clock. So you probably thought that nothing was the matter. But there was something the matter. Something very important. For, in reality, it was still only nine-thirty. Do you realise what nine-thirty meant? It was still over ten minutes before Yuki Konno would be killed at nine forty-two. Given the distance between White Wave Apartments and Takano Apartments, there was still plenty of time to go out and commit the murder. But in order to do so, Moro needed to have you remain alone in White Wave Apartments, while he found an excuse to go out. That's why he said he'd buy some drinks and snacks and left. I'm repeating myself, but that happened at around nine-thirty. Let's call that stage five.

'And now we come to the act of murder itself. Moro made his way to Takano Apartments, making sure nobody would notice him. I don't know what excuse he gave, but he made his way into Yuki Konno's flat. Perhaps he had already arranged to see her there that evening. Anyway, he stabbed her to death. At nine forty-two he threw her body from the balcony and fled the scene. I don't think I need to explain why he threw her dead body from the balcony, do I? In order for Moro's alibi to hold, he needed the time of Yuki Konno's death to be incontrovertible. That was the sixth stage.

'But there was still an important task awaiting Moro, even after finishing his murder. He needed to return to White Wave Apartments as quickly as possible. And in reality, he did commit the murder at nine forty-two, and returned to White Wave Apartments at nine forty-five. The clock on the video deck would be indicating ten-fifteen when Moro reappeared in front of you, slightly out of breath. Do you know why? Shiki, you understand why? Especially for us, this has a special meaning.'

Shiki mumbled a vague reply whilst he was considering the options.

'Well, err, don't all murderers try to flee the scene of the crime as quickly as possible...'

'Yes, but that's too commonplace. There's another reason Moro raced back as fast as he could to White Wave Apartments. For it's as clear as day that before long, the vicinity of Takano Apartments would be swarming with police cars.'

Shiki still didn't seem to understand the point his boss was making.

'Why would he be so afraid of police cars? It's not as if the police would be able to find the killer as soon as they arrived. He'd only attract more attention by running away.'

'True enough. But Moro wasn't afraid of the police cars.'

'Huh? I don't get it.' Shiki gave up.

'What do you mean?' Ryūhei also wanted an explanation.

'It's simple. He was afraid of the *sirens* of the police cars. That was the greatest hurdle in his murderous scheme. He had tampered with your sense of the time by showing you a shortened version of the film and by moving the clock on the video deck. But what if you had, even faintly, heard the sound of police sirens? It would all have been over at that very moment. The very first police car to arrive at the scene of the crime two evenings ago actually happened to be driven by Shiki and me, and we arrived at nine forty-eight. Other police cars arrived after us as well. You thought it was thirty minutes later than it actually was, so if you had heard the noises of the sirens, you would have

146

thought you'd heard them at ten-eighteen. But then, if you read the newspaper reports the following day, the exact time of death of nine forty-two would probably be given. How could the fall have occurred at nine forty-two, but the police cars not arrive until ten-eighteen, you would have asked yourself. And, unless you really are dim-witted, you would eventually realise the truth. Moro wanted to avoid that whole scenario. So what did he do? There was only one way. He had to return to White Wave Apartments before the police cars assembled at the crime scene. And keep you inside the home theatre. The home theatre is sound-proof, so you wouldn't have been able to hear the police sirens from inside. Moro could even have switched the stereo on to play hard rock if he had really wanted to play it safe, and then you definitely wouldn't have been able to hear any noise from outside. And that's exactly what Moro did. Stage seven completed.

'You didn't suspect a thing and didn't hear the sirens, so you started drinking with Moro. The drinks and snacks he brought had, of course, been purchased earlier, because the fifteen minutes before your party certainly hadn't been used to buy groceries. He had probably put everything in a bag of Hanaoka Liquors beforehand and hidden it in one of the kitchen cupboards. He retrieved it on his return and pretended he had just bought it all. And so you started on the drinks together. It was necessary for Moro to chat and drink with you for the next fifteen minutes. It was possible that, outside of the home theatre, you might hear the noise of police sirens. So he couldn't allow you to put even one foot outside the home theatre. And he couldn't just make you drink silently, so that's why he had to chat with you. And, it needed to be about something interesting enough to keep you in the room.

'The conversation turned out to be a very delicate affair. After all, going by the clock on the video deck, Moro had left his flat at ten o'clock, and had returned fifteen minutes later, having visited Hanaoka Liquors. But they were no ordinary fifteen minutes, because a murder had occurred at Takano Apartments at nine forty-two. Which meant that the fifteen minutes between ten o'clock and ten-fifteen were precisely when countless policemen, police cars, and onlookers would have been gathered in front of Takano Apartments, just at the time that Moro would have supposedly been passing by to get the groceries. Now, imagine the scene if Moro, returning to his flat, had failed to mention that something had happened at Takano Apartments. Wouldn't that have seemed weird? That's why Moro had to pretend that he had just witnessed a scene when he went out.'

147

Ryūhei looked confused.

'Wa—wait, so that means… doesn't that mean he was talking about something that hadn't even occurred yet!?'

'Exactly. Moro was simply imagining what the scene at Takano Apartments would look like between ten o'clock and ten-fifteen when he told you about it between nine forty-five and ten, so in a sense he was talking future events. It was a very risky thing to do, which is why he didn't talk about it in detail and was deliberately vague. Like how there were a lot of police cars, or that a crowd had formed. That was all he could say.'

'Aha, now that you point it out to me….'

'That was the eighth stage of the murder. We're almost reaching the finale.'

Sunagawa was getting deeper into his explanation as he went on.

'The clock in the home theatre would have been indicating a time of ten-thirty when the eighth stage was completed. In reality, it was still ten o'clock. And you can guess what Moro had to do next. He now needed to go out to buy a second lot of snacks and drinks at Hanaoka Liquors. He needed to make sure that the testimonies of Tomura inside the home theatre, and the boss of Hanaoka Liquors outside, would match up. So Moro once again needed an excuse to leave the room on his own. So what was his reason? He was going to take a shower. Moro's excuse may have sounded a bit unnatural, but he declared he was going to take a shower right then. And Tomura here could hardly tell him not to. So Moro left the home theatre once again alone. He pretended he was going to taking a shower and even turned the shower on, but in reality he left the flat. It was a complete coincidence that Akemi Ninomiya was working on her motorcycle outside. Moro passed her saying he was going to the liquor store. He went to the shop and bought drinks and snacks. He of course was careful in picking what he'd buy. He needed to buy two bottles of Kiyomori sake and two cans of *chūhai*. Fried rice crackers, potato crisps, salami slices, you know the list. And acting completely normally, he also started some small talk with the owner there about what had happened across the street at Takano Apartments. He joined the crowd, where he found the chef of Kōreiken and talked with him as well.'

Shiki immediately had a question ready.

'But why did he need to go around talking with everyone? I suppose talking with the boss of the liquor store was natural, but wasn't the chat with the chef of Kōreiken unnecessary?'

'No, that was necessary too. Remember that when Moro talked with Tomura here (stage eight), Moro told him he had mingled with the crowd and that he ran back after sticking around for a while? That was an excuse he came up with, because he had sprinted back to his flat so Tomura would not hear the police sirens arriving at the crime scene. But because of that excuse, Moro needed to actually have mingled with the crowd for a while. So at stage eight Moro had to speak about the future to a certain degree, and now he had to act according to his own story. He did things exactly the other way around. Usually, you do something and then tell somebody about it. Moro however had to act the same way he had told Tomura about earlier. So Moro had to find someone who would confirm that he had indeed mingled with the crowd. That person was the owner of Kōreiken. And after his chat with the chef, Moro decided to head home straight away.

'At the entrance gate he would see Akemi Ninomiya again. That would happen around ten-fifteen. He would sneak back into his flat, get back in the bathroom, take a quick shower, and return to Tomura with a wet head. That would also help him hide his perspiration and any quickness of breath. That would be at ten-seventeen or eighteen. The clock in the home theatre would say ten forty-seven or eight. At worst, you'd only think he'd had a long shower, but you'd never dream he had gone out. You'd believe he had been in the shower all that time. That would have completed stage nine. Basically everything that had to be done, would have been accomplished.'

Sunagawa slowly moved to the climax of his story.

'Stage ten would have been simple. He would offer you more drinks, and wait till you were drunk. Of course he'd make sure you wouldn't be so far gone so you wouldn't remember anything. Once you were asleep, he'd turn the digital clock in the home theatre back to the correct time. And then the whole thing would have been over and done.'

Then Sunagawa added a sentence which pierced the tense atmosphere in the interrogation room.

'But Moro never made it to that stage, because he died.'

6

The shocking truth had been revealed. But was it the whole truth? Kōsaku Moro had killed Yuki Konno. There was no more doubt about it at this point. And it was also true that he had fabricated an alibi to accomplish that goal. But the intricately planned scheme had collapsed before it could be completed, due to the killer's own death. Only one half of the truth had been revealed.

Ryūhei felt as though he was about to be flayed alive.

'You can't think that I was the one who killed Moro during the execution of his plan!? That Moro killed Yuki and that I killed Moro....'

'I did consider that idea, of course,' said Sunagawa, as he looked out of the window. It was already dark outside.

'But you didn't have a motive for killing him. Don't forget, we first suspected you as the killer of Yuki Konno. We thought Moro was your accomplice, and that you two had had a falling out. But if Moro was the murderer of Yuki Konno, then I couldn't think of a reason for you to kill him. And your story of the locked door chain also contradicted the idea of you being his killer. Because it was unthinkable that you'd tell us a story that only made you look more guilty.'

Chief Inspector Sunagawa's explanation of the truth had been very smooth up to that point, but he appeared to have lost his momentum. He didn't seem to have a full grasp of the truth any more.

'You see, we were convinced that you, and only you, were the killer. And there's nobody among the other suspects who seems likely to have killed him.'

Shiki asked his boss with a note of irritation in his voice: 'So does that mean it's back to the drawing board for the investigation of the Kōsaku Moro murder?''

'Yes.'

'Meaning we'll have to go through the list of suspects again?'

'We hadn't really looked into his work relations yet.'

'Or the women in his life.'

'That, too. Anyway, it's back to zero for us.'

'Chief Inspector, I don't think that'll be necessary.'

Somebody had suddenly spoken up, as if he had been waiting all along for Sunagawa to finish. It was the person whose presence in the room everyone had almost forgotten.

'Don't worry,' said Ukai as he raised his hand. 'I have some ideas about the identity of the murderer.'

'Ha!' Sunagawa exclaimed with interest. 'Are you going to confess?'

'I'm absolutely not joking.'

The private detective emphasised how serious he was, but the two police detectives were clearly not impressed. Shiki even started to play along, so as to make a fool of Ukai.

'Well then, please tell us. Saves us some trouble, right, sir?'

'Yes indeed,' Sunagawa agreed. 'Why don't you tell us about your ideas, hmm?'

There was a moment's silence. Ryūhei waited anxiously for the detective to speak.

'I'm afraid I can't tell you who the killer is right now.'

Disappointment. Ryūhei immediately regretted having brought the case to his attention. He was supposed to be a detective, but all he had done so far was to listen to Chief Inspector Sunagawa's great deductions. You almost felt sorry for him.

'However, Chief Inspector, if you give me about thirty minutes, I can lead the way to the one and only final solution. How about it?'

Wait, now was not the time for sympathy.

'Err, Mr. Ukai, a moment please?'

Ryūhei furiously pulled Ukai into a corner of the interrogation room.

'Wha—wha—what are you doing? Why are you making such promises? You're only making me feel embarrassed for you.'

But Ukai would not be stopped. 'Mind your words, Kid. And stop feeling embarrassed. You and that police detective might not be able to see the truth behind this case, but I can, better than anyone else. So just sit down and watch what's coming.'

Ryūhei felt anxious. He may have escaped one disaster, but he felt that further turmoil lay ahead.

7

Ryūhei eventually found himself sitting in the backseat of a police car. Ukai was sitting next to him, leaning forward as he gave directions. 'Right at that corner,' 'Go left there,' etc. Shiki was behind the wheel. He was irritated and drove wildly, making the two in the back seat sway left and right. He groaned: 'I'm a cop, I know the way. We're going to Nishisaiwai Bridge, aren't we? You don't need to tell me the way at each and every corner.'

Shiki had been right. Their police car was indeed headed for Nishisaiwai Bridge through the darkened streets of Ikagawa City. Sunagawa, who was sitting in the passenger's seat, turned around.

'Is there something on the bridge? Or in the river?'

'I can't tell you yet.'

Private detectives always play coy. Ukai was no exception.

Naturally, Ryūhei had an idea of where Ukai was taking them. Kinzō and his cardboard home were beneath Nishisaiwai Bridge. Kinzō had come up with the spear theory. But what did he have to do with the murder? Ryūhei was both curious and uneasy about what was about to happen.

Ukai probably had his own pride to think of. His pride as a private detective must have been wounded when Chief Inspector Sunagawa unveiled the mystery of the fabricated alibi in front of them. Ukai probably wanted to solve the final remaining mystery himself, and show the two police detectives what he was made of....

How childish!

Eventually, the police car arrived at Nishisaiwai Bridge. The private detective told Shiki to park the car near the bank. He then addressed the police detectives in front: 'Could you let me and Tomura go alone from here on, Chief Inspector?'

'No!' Sunagawa was not that understanding a man.

'Pfeh, how petty.' Ukai wasn't the obedient type.

'You don't have to look so unhappy. The suspicions regarding your own role haven't been cleared completely just yet. Don't forget that.'

'Okay,' Ukai gave in. 'But keep a ten-metre distance then, and keep out of it. You're experts in tailing people, after all. Let's go.' And he pushed Ryūhei out of the car.

'Keep out of it? Boss, did you hear him!?' protested Shiki.

'Don't you start crying, too. Just watch what he's going to do.'

Ukai quickly climbed down the bank to the riverside as he listened to the background music of an irate Shiki and a pacifying Sunagawa talking things over. Ryūhei followed Ukai's trail. When both of them had climbed down, they turned around to see the police detectives were indeed keeping their distance and hiding about ten metres behind them. That was pretty creepy on its own.

'I'd have preferred it if they were standing right behind us.'

'I wouldn't.'

Ukai didn't like other people's suggestions. Ryūhei didn't push the matter further.

The moon was hidden. The light from the city only illuminated the night sky, not the sunken riverside, where there was almost complete darkness. The only sounds Ryūhei could hear were the footsteps of the police detectives behind him, and the running water of the Ika River nearby. Occasionally he could hear a car crossing the Nishisaiwai Bridge overhead, but that only made things feel even creepier.

They made their way through the high grass to arrive at the base of the bridge. In the darkness they could spot the curious form of a cardboard house. It was Kinzō's home. A restless, strange feeling overcame Ryūhei, as he looked at the place where he had spent the previous night.

It was at this point that Ryūhei wanted to know what Ukai was planning.

'Wait. What is the meaning of this? Do you need something from Kinzō?'

'Just stay still and see.'

Ukai didn't answer Ryūhei's questions and headed straight for Kinzō's home.

Just as the day before, a sheet of plywood was leaning against one of the walls of the cardboard home, serving as the front door. Ukai raised his right hand to knock.

'Hey, Kinzō, are you there?'

Ukai moved the plywood board and looked inside. Ryūhei also peered inside, from behind Ukai. As he had expected, it was too dark inside to make out anything, but there was no answer, so it didn't appear anyone was there.

'Huh, not at home.'

'So, what now? Are we going to wait?'

Ukai didn't answer as he replaced the plywood board in its original position. He walked around the cardboard house to the rear. There was another cardboard house there. It appeared its owner was at home. A faint light was visible through the gaps in the cardboard.

'Where's the entrance? Oh, here it is.'

Ukai looked at the blue plastic sheet in front of him. It had been draped across the roof of the home and covered the entrance. It was a very simple, makeshift entrance. Ukai tapped on the sheet, making a dull sound. Would that gesture really be understood as knocking on the door? Whilst Ryūhei was still wondering about that, the blue plastic sheet was raised from within. The person inside showed himself.

'Why are you bothering me? Want something?' said a hoarse voice.

There was an accent to the voice, but it was not clear what kind of accent it was. The face was also not clearly visible due to the darkness. His miserable appearance was as to be expected from a homeless person. It was also clear that he had been homeless for quite some time. But Ryūhei knew that he had never seen or met the man before. Ukai immediately started talking to him.

'Forgive me for being so blunt, mister, but did you stab someone two nights ago? It would have happened somewhere around Saiwaichō Park?'

Ryūhei was astonished by Ukai's brazen question. He didn't know how Ukai had arrived at his conclusion, but who would dare to ask a person they had never met before if they had stabbed someone? Ryūhei was ready for there to be trouble and he stiffened his back, but the mysterious man smiled and didn't seem to mind at all.

'Huh, how do you know that? You don't look like a cop? But yes, as you said, I did stab some young fellow two evenings ago. But let me tell you, I'm no killer! I'm just a poor thief!'

The man in front of them had apparently just confessed he was the culprit, yet he showed no sign of running away. Still, the things he said sounded completely foreign to Ryūhei.

'Detectives, hey, over here!'

'What's going on? What's over there?'

The two police detectives answered Ukai's call and emerged out of the darkness.

The homeless person did not resist and crawled out of his cardboard house. He stood with a slightly arched back.

'What's the meaning of this?' Chief Inspector Sunagawa asked Ukai.

'Allow me to introduce you to the gentleman who stabbed Kōsaku Moro,' said Ukai, as he pointed to the man with the arched back.

'What!' Sunagawa took a good look at the man and asked the private detective a perfectly reasonable question.

'Who is this guy?'

Ukai shrugged ostentatiously.

'Don't ask me. I don't know his name. As to his occupation... well, as you can see for yourself, he's homeless.'

'What? And yet you claim that this man whose name you don't even know is the killer?'

'Why not? I'm not S.S. Van Dine. And who cares about his name or occupation? If you really want to know, ask him yourself. Anyway, Chief Inspector, I have just handed you the true murderer of Kōsaku Moro.'

The private detective looked triumphant as he spoke those words.

Nobody knew what was going on, but apparently the case was closed. Ryūhei was utterly baffled.

8

The mysterious man from the cardboard house confessed his crimes frankly to the police detectives and they cuffed him. And, with that, there was no further excuse to keep Ukai and Ryūhei in police custody, so the two of them were released on the spot.

'We might still need you for some questions, so don't suddenly disappear again.'

The Chief Inspector did not forget to make that clear to the duo. Shiki still didn't understand what was going on, but he led the homeless man they had arrested to their car. The two police detectives and one culprit drove off.

As Ryūhei looked at the taillights disappearing into the distance, it finally hit him that the feverish nightmare of the last three days had finally ended.

However, reality did not begin the moment the nightmare was over. Ryūhei still had a mountain of unanswered questions, so he still couldn't quite believe it

The two returned to the Morio Ukai Detective Agency by taxi. As soon as they reached the office, Ryūhei asked Ukai for an explanation. Why did that homeless person they didn't even know stab Moro to death? How did Ukai know that? Why didn't the homeless person resist his capture?

'Oh, that's very simple.'

Ukai made himself comfortable on his couch as he started his explanation. Ryūhei sat down on the chair opposite the couch. In front of them were two cups of steaming hot coffee. The detective took a sip of his coffee and stuck his right hand in the pocket of his jacket in search of something. When the hand appeared again, there was a brownish shell-like object between its fingers.

'What does this look like to you?'

'A pistachio?' Ryūhei cocked his head.

'Exactly. The shell of a pistachio nut. It's the one I found in the home theatre when the two of us examined Moro's flat yesterday. When I picked it up, I never guessed that it would solve the case.'

'That shell solved the case? How?'

'Think about it carefully. Why was this pistachio shell lying inside the home theatre? For example, could it be that the room wasn't clean, and it had been lying there for over a week?'

Ryūhei denied that possibility immediately.

'No way. It's from the evening before yesterday. It's from when Moro and I were drinking in the home theatre. Among the snacks he bought were pistachios. One of those shells must have fallen on the floor, and you picked it up.'

Ukai nodded.

'That is, of course, what happened. And what does that tell us? It tells us something about the contents of the bag of groceries from Hanaoka Liquors which Moro brought in two nights ago. According to you, the bag contained two bottles of the refined sake Kiyomori. Two cans of *chūhai*. Peanuts and small crescent-shaped fried rice crackers. Potato crisps. Salami slices. Cheese *tara* (cheese & cod sticks). And pistachios. But you didn't go into detail about which snacks you opened and which were left untouched, in the fifteen minutes you spent together drinking and chatting. And I didn't ask you about it, either. But it's clear that you *did* open the bag of pistachios then. And that's why there was a shell lying on the floor.'

'Yes, that's right. So what?'

'Not "so what"!' Ukai made fun of Ryūhei's failure to keep up.

'Don't you get it? Over the course of this case, the two of us saw that plastic bag from Hanaoka Liquors twice. Once when you were drinking with Moro two nights ago. The following day, you threw it into a garbage can in Saiwaichō Park as you were fleeing the scene, in an attempt to destroy evidence. The bag was picked up by someone soon after you threw it away. I suspected it was one of the homeless people nearby. Do you remember?'

'Yes, I remember.'

'The second time we saw a Hanaoka Liquors bag was last night. I took you to Kinzō's place, and Kinzō opened a Hanaoka Liquors bag right before our eyes. It was as if the bag you had thrown away had miraculously found its way into Kinzō's home. And the contents were the same as well: two bottles of the refined sake Kiyomori, peanuts and small crescent-shaped fried rice crackers, potato crisps, salami slices, all of that. Considering that Kinzō had probably already consumed part of the contents, it's no mystery why the bag was lighter than when you threw it away. But there was one mystery. It was the fact that the bag of pistachios hadn't been opened yet. I know that for sure, because I had to open it myself.'

'Ah!'

Ryūhei finally realised what the contradiction was. Ukai had indeed pulled the pistachio bag out of the Hanaoka Liquors bag and opened it right in front of him. Which meant that it was still sealed at that time.

156

'And do you know what means?' Ukai challenged Ryūhei.

'It means that the Hanaoka Liquors plastic bag in Kinzō's possession was not the one I had thrown into the garbage can in Saiwaichō Park. There were two different bags.'

'Exactly. But how could that be? It would mean that there were two Hanaoka Liquors bags with the exact same contents. That couldn't possibly happen by chance. And that's why you need to think back to the trick that Chief Inspector Sunagawa explained to us. Moro had indeed used two separate bags from Hanaoka Liquors in order to execute his plan.'

Ukai took another sip from his coffee before he continued.

'Let's go over this to make things clear. After you finished watching *Massacre Manor,* Moro went out, saying he was going to buy drinks and snacks. In truth, he went out to kill Yuki Konno, but he couldn't let you know that, so he had already prepared a bag from Hanaoka Liquors, which he brought with him when he returned to join you in the home theatre. That's the bag you saw two nights ago. It was also the bag you disposed of the following morning. But the bag Kinzō had was a completely different one. So where did that second bag come from?'

'Kinzō said he got it from his neighbour…'

'Yes, from that anonymous homeless person. And how did he get hold of it?'

'…'

'Do you remember what Chief Inspector Sunagawa told us during his explanation of the trickery pulled by Moro? He said that, when Moro left you in the home theatre, he told you he was going to take a shower. But in reality, in order to fabricate his alibi, he went out to do some shopping at Hanaoka Liquors. He was careful about what he bought, so that your testimony wouldn't contradict the shop owner's. But then, strangely enough, this second bag disappeared. Where did it go? Did he throw it away on his way back? No, no, impossible. It's true that it was only a tool to fabricate his alibi, which he could throw away later, but he would never have thrown it away on the way back. Remember, he had greeted Akemi Ninomiya at the entrance of White Wave Apartments that night and had told her he was going to buy some drinks. So there was no way he was going to throw the plastic bag away and return home empty-handed, given that he was probably be going to see her again on his return. And yet the bag from Hanaoka Liquors did leave Moro's side, and it did come into the possession of our anonymous homeless person, and then Kinzō. What does that all mean?'

'I know! Moro was robbed of his bag! By the anonymous homeless person!'

'Yes. After shopping at Hanaoka Liquors, Moro mingled with the crowd and then headed back home, just as he had planned. Naturally he passed through Saiwaichō Park, as that's the shortest way. There a completely unanticipated incident occurred. A homeless person living in the park tried to steal the Hanaoka Liquors bag from him! I don't know if you still remember, but the night of the twenty-eighth of February was very chilly. The cold, trembling homeless person saw a young man carrying a bag with refined sake walking quickly, right past him. And at that very same moment, an evil thought crossed his mind.'

'He stabbed Moro and stole the bag.'

Surprisingly, Ukai's response was a strong denial.

'No, that's not what happened. That would have been murder during a robbery. But this was different. There wasn't any murder involved.'

No murder involved? The homeless man had said the same thing at the time of his arrest. "I'm no killer!" and "I'm just a poor thief!" he had protested.

'I think it was a legitimate case of self-defence. Theft is still theft, of course.'

'Self-defence!'

'The man had quite simply chosen the wrong target. All he wanted to do was snatch the bag and flee. What was the worst thing that could happen for stealing a bag of sake and snacks? But, for Kōsaku Moro, it wasn't just a bag of drinks and snacks. As I just explained, he knew there was a very high probability he'd see Akemi Ninomiya again at the front gate of White Wave Apartments, and it would be very dangerous to return home empty-handed. So he absolutely could not afford to let go of that bag of drinks and snacks. He was right in the middle of the final stages of his criminal plan. Why would he allow some homeless man to get in the way? I suspect he resorted to an extreme measure in order to protect the bag. He took out the knife he was carrying.'

'The knife he used to stab Yuki?'

'Yes. He'd already stabbed one person with it, so he wouldn't feel any compunction about doing it again. He didn't really intend to stab the man, of course. I think he just wanted to scare off someone who had suddenly appeared to steal his all-important bag. The homeless man, on the other hand, must have been completely taken aback. He could never have imagined that someone would brandish a knife against a simple bag snatcher. Moro and the homeless person started to struggle. And when it was all over, Moro ended up with his own knife in his right side.'

Ryūhci groaned as he imagined the ironic conclusion to the course of events.

'That's right, those police detectives did say that the wound in Yuki's back and the wound in Moro's side were very likely caused by the same weapon. That's why I became their suspect. But, in fact, the knife that Moro had used to kill Yuki killed him as well.'

'Precisely. Our homeless Nemo took the bag and ran away after stabbing Moro. I don't think I have to explain any further about what Moro did next. You have already been witness to my great deductions about that.'

'Huh? Great deductions? What great deductions?' Ryūhei was puzzled by Ukai's claim.

'Surely you're not going to make me repeat myself all over again? You know, the "internal bleeding inside a locked room" theory.'

'Aah! Oh, that brings me back. I'd already forgotten about that term.'

'Don't forget important things so easily. That theory is the only one which solves the mystery of the locked room. I said that from the very beginning, of course.'

And he was right. After Ryūhei had asked the private detective about his experience in locked room mysteries, Ukai had immediately proposed the "internal bleeding inside a locked room" theory. After hearing Akemi Ninomiya's testimony, he seemed to have abandoned it, but once he heard Chief Inspector Sunagawa explain the time-lag trick, his theory came alive again like a Phoenix. It was a good thing Ukai had clung so strongly to it.

'Moro visited Hanaoka Liquors a little after ten o'clock in the evening. So we can assume that he got into a struggle with the homeless man in Saiwaichō Park around ten past ten. Like the black man in *Proof of the Man*, Moro covered the wound in his right side with his coat and kept pressure on it with his right hand. He then started walking back to Flat 4 of White Wave Apartments. I don't know whether he actually knew what he was doing, or whether it was just an unconscious act. Akemi Ninomiya was still at the entrance, of course. Moro came in at around ten-fifteen, just as she told us. He didn't greet her, but just walked by. If she had paid a little more attention to him then, she might have noticed that his gait was unsteady, but she didn't see it. She even assumed he was holding a bag of groceries in his right hand at the time, because he was holding it at waist height. In reality, Moro's right hand was not holding a bag, but probably holding the knife handle beneath his coat. When Moro finally reached his flat, he locked the door chain of the front door himself. And lo and behold, the room was locked!'

Ukai made the declaration with a triumphant look on his face.

'The rest is simple. Moro took his coat off and put it on the coat hook in the entrance hall. He staggered in to the bathroom and pulled the knife from his right side. He must have died instantly, at around ten-seventeen or eighteen. And then you discovered his body. The clock in the home theatre would have indicated just after eleven, but in reality it was just after ten-thirty. Ten thirty-five, to be exact.'

'Huh? How do you know the exact time?' asked Ryūhei.

'Please try to keep up. Akemi Ninomiya told us. She heard the loud noise of something falling to the floor of the bathroom of Flat 4 at ten thirty-five. At first we mistakenly assumed that was the time Moro died, but we were wrong.'

'Ah! I get it!'

'Yes, the noise she heard was you fainting in the dressing room after you discovered Moro's body. You lost consciousness at ten thirty-five in the evening and didn't come round until the following morning.'

Ryūhei groaned again, thinking of how pathetic he had been.

'Hmmm. So if I hadn't fainted and had gone to the police immediately, I would have noticed that I was actually thirty minutes ahead in real time. And Moro's trickery would have been discovered right away. So, in the end, I was the one who made things so confusing.'

'Well, you could say that. But that wasn't all there was to it. You're forgetting that there was also one heck of a coincidence that played a role. A prank played by Heaven, you could call it. And it genuinely came from Heaven, too: the lightning.'

'The lightning!'

'While you were dozing that night, lightning struck in the vicinity of White Wave Apartments, causing a blackout. It reset the internal digital clock of the video deck. That was the tenth stage of Chief Inspector Sunagawa's explanation. Because of Moro's death, there was nobody there to actually execute that tenth stage, but by sheer coincidence, the lightning fulfilled the exact same role. If not for the lightning, we would have noticed that the clock of the video deck was running thirty minutes ahead when we visited the place the following day, and we would have arrived at the truth ourselves. Anyway, this curious locked room mystery only came to be because of several coincidences coming together.'

Ukai took the cup of coffee, now cold, and raised it, as if to drink a toast.

'Anyway, all's well that's ends well. We've finally managed to open our locked room. Oh, who's that? At this hour? Maybe they have the wrong number?'

The phone on the desk had suddenly started ringing. Ukai put his cup down, went over to the desk, and picked up the receiver.

'Well, well, a phone call from our brilliant Chief Inspector himself!' Even his attitude on the phone was not serious. It was indeed Chief Inspector Sunagawa on the phone.

'Oh, so our homeless man has confessed everything? Aha, that's good to hear. Did he say it was done in self-defence? What's that... how did I know? Haha, what kind of question is that? I know everything that's happened. No, no, you don't need to thank me. A commendation? Me? Hahaha, such an insignificant trifle? I'm not interested... I only work for the honour of my clients. Well then, Chief Inspector, till we meet again. Yes, goodbye.'

Ukai replaced the receiver noisily.

'...'

Ryūhei wanted to know what had been said, of course.

'Was that Chief Inspector Sunagawa?'

'Yes. The case ended exactly as I had expected. So that's good news.'

'Yes. But err, that commendation, is that like one of those....'

'Sure. Some high-ranking person gives you a certificate and some commemorative item.'

'You declined.'

'Of course. It's against my policy to obsess about awards and stuff.'

'What a waste.'

'No, not at all. I didn't help the police in order to receive trinkets.'

'But why not accept it for the time being?'

'...'

'Mr. Ukai.'

'What?'

'Aren't you also thinking right now that you shouldn't have said no?'

'…'

Silence. But then the private detective seemed to be over it, or at least he tried to hide his regret from Ryūhei. He laughed out loud.

'Hahahahahaha, that's a nice joke. I'm a private detective. What would I do with a certificate from my business rivals! There's nothing worse you could do to a man than to award him with a commendation! Hahahahaha!'

It was in fact a curious attitude, and his unnaturally long laugh betrayed the fact that his true feelings on the matter were quite different. Perhaps it was a glimpse of what a "proud man walking the dirty streets" should look like.

9

'So I told him he might get a commendation.'

'Huh, he must have been happy to hear that.'

'He said he didn't want it.'

'He said no? Wow. His pride as a private detective speaking?'

'Probably,' said Sunagawa, but he didn't forget to make sure Shiki did his work. 'Eyes on the screen. This is very important work.'

The night during which the case had been cracked had turned into dawn. It was the morning of the third of March. Chief Inspector Sunagawa and Shiki were in Flat 4 of White Wave Apartments and working hard to secure more evidence for their case. Their current task: the immense number of video tapes that covered the shelves on the wall of the home theatre. If Sunagawa's reasoning was correct, the tape with the two-hour version of *Massacre Manor* should still be hidden amongst them. That was what logic dictated, but actually finding it was turning out to be a tough job. It was impossible to tell in which area of the shelves Kōsaku Moro had hidden it. Needless to say, it would have been easy if the tape had been clearly labelled, but that was not likely to be the case, quite the contrary. It was very probable that, in order to camouflage the tape, it had a label that said something completely different. There was therefore only one thing to do for the detectives: play each and every tape in the video deck. Shiki focused on the job at hand, reasoning that they must eventually find it, even if it took a while. It was just a mindless repetition of boring and simple actions. Perhaps perfect for the morning after solving a case.

'Don't you feel like helping out too, sir? As you look at your diligent subordinate?'

'Not at all. The case is already solved.'

The Chief Inspector sitting in the middle of the room watching Shiki work. Yesterday, he was the brilliantly impressive Chief Inspector Sunagawa, but today he had reverted to his usual, work-shy self. He was the type who could focus on cracking an alibi, but who wouldn't feel like doing much to actually find supporting evidence.

'Sir, you say the case is solved, but I still have some questions.'

'Shoot. I'll answer them all. I don't have anything to do anyway.'

Shiki pouted his lips 'But I have plenty to do… Anyway, what I wanted to know concerns the night of the murder. Moro was talking with the owner of Kōreiken outside Takano Apartments when he saw me, and the expression on his face changed. What did he see to give him such a shock?'

'Oh, that. Surely, now that you know the trick he was playing at the time, it becomes self-evident. It was the sight of police detective Shiki which surprised him. Of course, to Kōsaku Moro, you didn't look like that.'

'Huh? What do you mean?'

'It's simple. Shiki, think back about how you were dressed on the day the murder happened.'

'Ah, I was dressed rather unusually.'

Shiki felt a bit ashamed as he finally recalled that he'd been dressed like some kind of hooligan turned low-level gangster.

'Think about it from Moro's point of view. How could he have guessed that a classmate from high school he hadn't met in years and dressed like that was, in fact, a police detective? Think what you looked like to him. Don't forget you were a bad apple in high school. Moro probably assumed that the hooligan Shiki had become an actual gang member in the last few years. And you were standing there talking with a patrol officer at the scene of the crime. What did the situation look like to him? The answer is simple, when you think about it.'

There was only one possible interpretation.

'Ah! He must have thought I was being treated as a suspect in the murder case!'

'Which was only natural. And it must have greatly disturbed the actual murderer himself, Moro. What's more, the circumstances didn't permit Moro to greet you and spend a few minutes chatting about the old days. As I explained yesterday, Moro had spoken to Tomura about events in the future and he was obliged to act according to what he'd told him. His face betrayed how upset and utterly shocked he must have been to see you, but in the end he decided to ignore you. And that, of course, looked very unnatural to you. That's all there was to it.'

Shiki nodded at the Chief Inspector's explanation. Given that Moro himself was the killer, his reaction to Shiki was only natural. On the other hand, Shiki himself could not possibly have imagined that Moro was the murderer. Which is why Moro's reaction was such a mystery to him.

'There's one more thing I don't understand.'

'Motive, yes? Why did he need to kill Yuki Konno? That's our final problem. But….'

Chief Inspector Sunagawa yawned ostentatiously and seemed a bit annoyed at the question.

'What difference does it make now if we find out what his motive was? Moro himself is dead and he'll never be able to confirm or deny whatever theory we come up with. What does it matter? I don't see the point in spending too much energy on the question.'

Shiki didn't seem to like Sunagawa's response much.

'No, I had a different question, actually. I wanted to know why Moro went through so much trouble to fabricate his alibi. You could call it the motive for faking his alibi. That's what I don't get.'

'Aha, I see what you mean.'

Apparently, Chief Inspector Sunagawa had the same question on his mind. That reassured Shiki, and he continued.

'Usually, a murderer fakes their alibi as a means of avoiding suspicion, precisely because they are in a position that attracts suspicion. But when it came to the murder of Yuki Konno, it was highly unlikely that any suspicion would have fallen on Moro anyway. And yet he came up with a meticulously planned scheme to create an alibi for himself. It was only due to an unforeseen obstacle that it failed, and he got stabbed to death himself. I just don't get it. He was so smart, and to have that plan backfire at him in that manner…'

'Hmm, you're not wrong there,' muttered the Chief Inspector, but then he suddenly noticed something .

'Hey! Shiki! Look! What's that on the screen!?'

Shiki had been repeating the actions of inserting a tape, pushing the play button and ejecting the tape mindlessly, so Sunagawa's sudden interest came as a shock. He stared at the screen and saw a naked, uncensored woman… no, wait. Shiki looked closer at the screen. The scene was a bathroom. The image was unclear due to the rising steam. It was the back of a naked person. But it was definitely a man. A young man.

'What's that video?'

'It looks as though it was shot with a hidden camera. But he was filming a naked man… Aaah! Aaaaaaaah!'

'Really! Aaah!'

The two police detectives shouted out simultaneously.

'But that's Ryūhei Tomura!!'

They discovered more tapes with Ryūhei Tomura in his birthday suit. Ryūhei had simply seen Moro as a senior from college. But perhaps Moro had seen Ryūhei as more than simply a junior. If so, it would become necessary to take another look at the case with that in mind.

Chief Inspector Sunagawa thought about it for a long time and made a pronouncement based on their shocking discovery.

'It seems pretty clear that Moro probably killed Yuki Konno on behalf of Tomura.'

'On behalf of?'

'I don't mean they were accomplices. Do you remember how Tomura made a scene at the train station one night, after the shock of being dumped by Yuki?'

'Do you mean the scene that student Yūji Makita told us about?'

'Yes. Because it was at the station, a lot of people were witness to it. So it's very likely that Moro heard about it, one way or another.'

'So, Moro decided to take revenge on Yuki for the sake of Tomura?'

'If you put it that way, yes. Tomura of course didn't hate Yuki Konno so much he wanted to kill her, even if she did break up with him. But even we at one time believed that Tomura hated her guts so much he killed her. Moro believed it as well. He believed that Tomura deeply loathed her, and so he decided to kill her, on behalf of his friend. I strongly suspect that to be the motive behind this case.'

'Tomura's hatred became his hatred. And he expressed his love in a twisted manner.'

'That's about it. And that puts a different light on the fabricated alibi of Moro.'

'How so?'

'It's just as you asked me. Moro had no motive to create a fake alibi for himself. That means that the fabricated alibi wasn't for himself. It was always meant to protect the person most likely to become a suspect for the murder of Yuki Konno: Ryūhei Tomura.'

'Wow! So it was all in order to provide Tomura with an alibi?' asked Shiki in surprise.

'Yes. Moro killed Yuki Konno for Tomura's sake. But he couldn't allow Tomura to become a suspect. So Moro planned and executed a scheme where he would commit the murder, whilst simultaneously providing Tomura with an alibi. If everything had gone as planned, Tomura would have come to us and testified that he had an alibi for the murder, as he had been watching a film with Moro. Doesn't it all fit now? Ah, what a dreadful tale! Of course, there's no way we'll be able to prove it.'

A little while later they found the tape with the short version of *Massacre Manor*. Chief Inspector Sunagawa's guess had been proved correct, and thus his whole line of reasoning was likely to be the truth.

But they never found any evidence to support their theory about the motive, so nobody would ever know whether Chief Inspector Sunagawa's assumptions were correct or not.

EPILOGUE

So now it seems as though all the mysteries in our story have been solved. Any further additions would be considered redundant, so I should really refrain from doing so, but allow me to write in a bit more detail about certain matters.

Some might be curious as to the fate of the anonymous homeless person. He, of course, was taken to court. The main issue at his trial was whether he should be tried for murder or for legitimate self-defence. The complex matter was deliberated upon for a long time, and in the end the court took the middle ground (the judge didn't say that, of course): the man was sentenced for excessive self-defence. Most agreed that legitimate self-defence was not appropriate because it was the defendant who had tried to rob the victim. He was given a suspended sentence. Needless to say, he couldn't return to his cardboard house, and has now been placed in the proper facility.

Chief Inspector Sunagawa and Shiki were not given promotions or any honorary ranks for their role in solving the case, and continue to serve the government. If you happen to spot a middle-aged man in a suit sitting by the canal behind the Ikagawa City Police Station and staring at the water and the sky above, that's probably Chief Inspector Sunagawa. But mind you, he might be busy cracking an alibi with that brain of his. It's best to not disturb him.

One can't help but feel sorry for Ryūhei Tomura. Perhaps it's best to leave him alone. But I do think it's important to record that there have been many sightings of him praying at the grave of Yuki Konno on top of a hill overlooking the sea. The greatest victim of this case was obviously Yuki, but the person who was hurt second-most was without a doubt Ryūhei Tomura.

Private detective Ukai was never contacted again about any commendations. Whilst he did feel he had let the opportunity slip away, he was a positive person and he believed he'd get a second chance. When that day came, he would gratefully accept the monetary award, even if he wasn't so sure about what to do with any certificates. But in order for that to happen, he needed to come across another case of the same calibre. He decided to rethink his marketing strategy. If you look in the yellow pages of Ikagawa City now, you're likely to find the ad "WELCOME TROUBLE" printed in larger letters than before. If you're interested, try calling the number. He's a rather picky detective though, so he might not be interested in small troubles.

The scene of the tragedy, White Wave Apartments, was demolished and does not exist anymore. The owner, Akemi Ninomiya, would later tell how the operator of the excavator was puzzled when he noticed that one room had extremely thick walls. He could probably never have guessed what the room had been used for.

CPSIA information can be obtained
at www.ICGtesting.com
Printed in the USA
LVHW080047280221
680113LV00013B/1174

9 798568 497219